for Barry — Many,
many thanks,
an author — at last!
Peg 3.04

Lizzie
at Last

A Novel

Margaret
Slaven

Full Court Press
Englewood Cliffs, New Jersey

First Edition

Copyright © 2003 by Margaret Slaven

Published in the United States of America
by Full Court Press, 601 Palisade Avenue,
Englewood Cliffs, NJ 07632.

ISBN 0-9752633-0-7

*Cover photograph, "Reflection," Copyright © Sterne Slaven 2003
Cover, book design, and author photograph by Barry Sheinkopf
Colophon design by Liz Sedlack*

FOR JAKE

"The first hope in our inventory—the hope that includes and at the same time transcends all others—must be the hope that love is going to have the last word."

—Arnold J. Toynbee,
Conditions of Survival

ACKNOWLEDGMENTS

The sun shone and a new life began for me—at this late stage in my life—the day I entered The Writing Center. I am ever grateful to Barry Sheinkopf for editing this book, but especially for his guidance and encouragement. My appreciation of my fellow seminar members is boundless. Blessings on my readers, Linda Mohr and my sister Adelaide Kern, who have for a very long time given me the gift of their support and good humor. Thanks also to the Reverend Kenneth Near and Dr. Jean McNally for their special help. I indeed have a grateful heart.

1

DEATH

IT WASN'T A GOOD NIGHT. The air had a runaway pulse to it, always an unhealthy condition in a hospital. There were too many patients in the ER, too many dropped dinner trays, too many codes over the intercom. Calm had moved out for the night, probably due to the storm, arriving in the darkness of late afternoon, barreling in from the west and blanketing the area with ice and snow and the misery of a howling wind.

Steve Heller jabbed at the up button for the East Wing elevator. He had patients to see, he was hungry, and his car had nearly slid into an intersection when he braked for a light on the way over from his office. Now the elevators weren't cooperating.

When he finally reached three, Sheila Ruben bumped into him.

Literally. A pediatrician whose practice was in the same building as Steve's, she appeared distracted and tense, lab coat buttoned wrong, wiry gray hair flying.

"Sorry—not looking where I'm going," she said as they knelt and together gathered the charts she had dropped.

"It's okay. You all right?"

She shook her head. "No. I'm losing a baby, and I'm sick about it." They entered the nurses' station, nodding to Sara Cunningham, an RN on duty, and Hildy Frye, an LPN.

"Newborn?"

"No, she's two. Bacterial meningitis."

"That's awful."

"And not the half of it. Absolutely beautiful child. The mother's already lost her husband. You remember, Bo Donnely? The state senator?" She ran a hand over her hair, causing even more disarray. "He was running for Congress when the plane he was in went down over the Pine Barrens?"

Steve looked up from the chart he had pulled. "Sure I remember. His wife's my patient. How is she?" He waved a hand. "No, forget it, wrong question. I can imagine how she is."

Sheila finished signing an order and replaced the chart. "Right. If we lose Katie. . . ." Her voice trailed off.

Steve watched her hurry down the hall towards the Peds ICU.

"She's a nice lady, too," Sara Cunningham said, reaching for the phone. "Mrs. Donnely."

"You're right, she is," Steve agreed.

"Pretty, too, and thin," Hildy added, glancing down at her fifty extra pounds.

"Right again." He shot Hildy a look, part sympathetic, part

amused. "Character's what counts, Hildy, and you've got plenty."

"Yeah, too much is what I'm thinking."

He grinned at her and headed into the medical ICU, putting Elizabeth Donnely and her pain out of his mind. Losing a spouse— he could write a book on that one, but the loss of a child. . .he didn't think he could handle that.

Back at the nurses' station he glanced up from writing orders and saw her coming down the hall. Elizabeth Donnely was slim and blonde and moved with an unstudied grace. Steve had never been able to figure out if her expression was one of aloofness or dis-trust. Tonight, however, she simply looked lost. She stopped at the counter that encircled the station.

"Mrs. Donnely," Steve said, "can I help you?" For a moment she didn't respond. *She probably feels as though someone has whacked her on the head with a two-by-four, and yet she's still standing.* He knew the feeling, had had it himself.

"Will you be here for awhile?" she asked.

"Twenty minutes or so. What can I do?"

"I'm looking for our priest."

"Sure. I'll keep an eye out."

He watched as she turned the corner to return to the ICU, saw her pause and put out a tentative hand to the wall for just a moment, before walking on. The memory of that gesture was to stay with him for weeks to come.

Steve didn't recognize the Donnelys' priest. Donnely—Roman Catholic, he figured. The woman approaching the station counter asking for Katie Donnely certainly didn't strike him as a priest. In a black parka over gray sweats, she looked more like a middle-aged gym teacher.

"I'm Annie West, the Donnelys' priest."

Steve, fighting the look of surprise that threatened to take over his features, introduced himself. "Yes, Mrs. Donnely was looking for you."

"She's here? Liz? I got an urgent message from her."

"Down that hall," he said, pointing. "Katie's in the pediatric ICU."

Later, all of his patients attended to, he made his way back to the third floor nurses' station. He knew as soon as he got off the elevator that Katie had died—solemn eyes that avoided looking at you, hushed voices, a lethargy that was rarely present in the ICU area. A child's death was a loss no one could feel a momentary sadness for and then move on. It got into the chest and hung there, a dead weight, going home with you at the end of your shift.

"Dr. Ruben?" he asked a nurse who had her head bent over a stack of orders.

"She left, Dr. Heller. Hard night for her."

"Christ," Steve sighed. "Mrs. Donnely?"

"Still down there. She has her priest with her."

"Tell me, women can be priests now?"

"Episcopalian."

"Oh, right," he said, feeling stupid.

At that moment Elizabeth Donnely and Annie West came down the hall toward the elevators. The priest, an arm around her parishioner's shoulders, was speaking intently to her, but Elizabeth's eyes were on something in the distance. She looked to Steve as though she was working too hard at holding herself together to be hearing much of anything. Seeing him, Annie West beckoned.

"Doctor, I'm trying to convince Mrs. Donnely that she can't drive home. Maybe you can make her understand how dangerous it would be. I want to call her a cab. I'd take her, but I couldn't get my car out of the driveway. I had to walk here from the rectory."

"Of *course* she can't. Mrs. Donnely, it's not a problem for me to drive you home. Actually, I think we live in the same town. And I'll have someone follow us in your car," he added quickly as she opened her mouth to protest.

He located a fellow in Food Service who had a break coming and was happy to earn twenty dollars to follow him. He'd drive the man back to the hospital. He also located some Valium. How did you sleep after losing your child? he wondered. For that matter, how did you put one foot in front of the other?

The snow came at them horizontally as they stepped out into the parking lot. Neither was wearing boots, and the footing was treacherous. After a couple of steps, Steve, like Annie West, realized that Elizabeth Donnely required support and put an arm around her. They struggled slowly toward his car, the snow icing their coats and hair, stinging their faces with its ferocity as they crossed the lot. The tall firs that separated the main road from the doctors' parking area resembled white monsters, bowing and threatening in the steady wind. When they reached his car at last, he settled her in the passenger seat and belted her in. He felt like a puppet master.

The wipers had to struggle to keep the windshield clear as the snow blew in billowing swoops, obstructing vision. Until he got used to the swerves and adjusted his braking and steering to allow for them, his attention was focused on the road. The fellow from Food Service stayed a good distance behind and seemed to be handling the ice.

They'd gone a couple miles before he glanced over at her. She was crying, the tears, bright in reflected lights, the only indication. No sound escaped her, but the tears were rolling nonstop down her cheeks. He took a hand off the wheel and reached into his breast pocket for a handkerchief.

"I can't *do* this," she said, her words barely audible as she took the handkerchief from him.

"Is someone at home? You won't be alone, will you?"

She shook her head, wiping the tears, but unable to keep up with them. "Angelica's there. She's with the boys."

The thought of her sons undid her. She hunched forward. Convulsive sobs shook her, such a presence in the dark closeness of the car that Steve could feel them searing the back of his throat. He reached a hand over and moved it in slow circles on her back, the only measure of consolation he could think to offer.

By the time they reached Aspenhill, she was quiet again, although tears continued to highlight her cheeks.

"It's the next left, Stelfox."

It was the old section of town, where there were sidewalks and homes with front porches and detached garages. She pointed to a large Victorian that sat back from the street, its porch light a beacon, and he pulled to the curb, waving the man in her car into the driveway.

The icing conditions were worsening rapidly as the night wore on and the temperature dropped. He held her close and they managed to reach the porch without falling. He remembered the envelope of pills, but she shook her head when he tried to give them to her.

"You have to sleep. Please, at least *take* them." He closed her fingers around the packet. "In case you change your mind. The first few days. . .you may need something to get through them."

She bent over, and he thought she was going to be sick. Just then the front door opened. The light from the globe on the porch ceiling shone on a young woman's worried face. Angelica, he supposed.

Elizabeth straightened and put a hand on his arm. For a moment he felt her weight against his body. Regaining her balance, she turned and went inside. The woman gave Steve a questioning look. He shook his head, and she closed the door.

2

PATIENT

"IT TAKES ORGANIZATION, Jen, organization and discipline, just to squeeze a doctor's appointment into my schedule." Liz Donnely leaned down and set the dogs' water bowl on the kitchen floor, taking care not to dislodge the phone, which she held firmly to an ear with a raised shoulder.

"Tell me again why you're going to see the doctor."

"Dizziness. It's getting so it makes me nauseous. I get up with it every morning, although it goes away as the day wears on. Believe me, I don't have time for a brain tumor."

"Oh, stop! How long's it been going on?"

Liz leaned over the sink and called through the open window, "Mickey!"

"Liz?"

"Sorry. I'm trying to get this dog. He knows I want him to come in, but he plays dumb." She rapped on the window. Mickey was standing in the middle of the yard wagging his tail. "Since the week-end, I think. So I decided I'd better do something about it. Listen, thanks for keeping Harry for me. I'll drop him off in about—" She looked up at the clock. "About fifteen minutes, and I shouldn't be too long, maybe an hour, an hour and a half?"

"That's fine. Harry's no trouble, you know that, and Ian will be thrilled he's coming. See you in fifteen."

The waiting room in the medical offices of Marini, Heller and Kaufman was crowded with patients. Glad that she'd brought work to do, Liz added her name to the sign-in list and found an unoccupied seat. She had written one report and was in the midst of another when she heard her name called.

After her weight, blood pressure, and pulse were recorded on her chart by a nurse, she was left to wait for Dr. Heller. She could hear his voice in the next room, a comforting voice for a doctor, unhurried and confident. She had sought him out a few years ago, after sitting beside him in the Port Smith Hospital conference hall during one of Bo's speeches. Months later, sick with bronchitis and unable to reach Bo's doctor, she'd recalled Dr. Heller's smile. Not a very clinical method of choosing a doctor she'd admit, but she found him an excellent diagnostician, as well as someone who was easy to talk to and so considered the choice a good one.

From her perch at the end of the examining table, she glanced around. Examining rooms had always intrigued her. Studying the garish posters of body organs and their pathologies, which decorated the walls, could occupy long minutes of waiting time. Whether they were designed to calm blood pressure was another matter. Then there were the labeled drawers that she longed to peer into but never did, and the murmuring voices from the hall and adjoining rooms with the occasional audible word or phrase that encouraged eavesdropping, all designed to make waiting bearable.

"Mrs. Donnely." Dr. Heller slipped quietly into the room. Hooking a stool with his foot, he pulled it closer to the examining table and lowered himself to its edge. "How are you?"

Tears hit the backs of her eyes with lightning speed. No lag time. "Here we are," they announced. "Try and act like a together person with us burning away back here." Four months since Katie's death, and the tears still appeared when she was least prepared for them. There seemed to be an unending supply, just waiting for a breach in her defense system. She blinked them back as best she could. The thing about Dr. Heller, she thought, was that he was expecting her to answer him. Lots of people asked the same question, but not too many listened to her reply.

"Functioning," she said. "Some days aren't so good, but I've gone back to work. And that helps." …But not much; it did force her to focus on her students and schedules, on IEP's and reports; it made it necessary for her to organize her and her boys' home life. But it hadn't wiped out grief. Grief—it seemed too gentle a word for the ferocious emotion that had taken up residence inside her, shaking her with storms of desire for what should have been and anger at what *had* been. If only she could box it off, deal with it in her own time and on her own terms. But it didn't work that way.

"…you've lost weight, but you'll gain it back," he was saying. "It takes time—sorry," he said, wincing, "I'm sure you're sick of hearing that." He gazed intently at her, tapping the edge of her chart in the palm of his hand. "Mrs. Donnely, I hope you'll agree to see my partner, Sam Kaufman. He's an excellent internist, and I think it will. . .I *know* it will work out," he said as he rose. "Wait one moment, will you?"

Liz stared at the closed door and was still staring when it reopened and a tall, sandy-haired man preceded Dr. Heller into the room. The two white coats faced her.

"This is Sam Kaufman. Sam, Elizabeth Donnely," and Dr. Heller backed out, pulling the door closed behind him.

"So it's not a brain tumor?"

"The farthest thing from it, Jen. Fluid in my middle ears. Probably an allergy now that spring's here, and everything's beginning to bloom. He gave me some antihistamines." She was standing in Jen's kitchen, jiggling the car keys. "Thanks for watching Harry. I really appreciate it."

"Wait! You haven't told me why the other guy walked out."

"That's what I don't know. He's the one who drove me home, you know, the night Katie—" She let the sentence hang. She still had trouble getting through that one.

"What night? Oh—I'm sorry, Liz."

"I know." Liz swallowed to ease the constriction in her throat. "Jen, I've tried to remember what happened on that ride, but it's a blur. I was out of my mind, I really can't remember much of anything."

"Yes, well, that's understandable. Why didn't you ask him— what's his name?"

"Heller."

"Why didn't you ask this Dr. Heller what his reason was for not seeing you?"

"I don't know. I guess I was too surprised. But as I was leaving, he came out of another exam room with a patient he was directing to X-ray."

"And? What happened? What'd you say?"

"Nothing. I just looked at him."

"You just looked at him? Fine. What was this, a silent movie?"

"No, there's more. He said, 'Mrs. Donnely, I owe you an explanation.' Then he waved his hand at all the activity and said, 'Would you mind if I called you?'"

"My Lord, this gets more and more interesting. What did you say?"

Liz shrugged. "What could I say?"

"So, go on, did he call?"

Liz gave her a look. "Jen, I haven't been home yet, have I?"

"Oh, this is true. Well, go." She went to the door to the family room and called, "Harry! Your mother's here!" Returning, she said, "And call me. I want to know what the big mystery is."

Liz was filling the dishwasher with dinner plates and utensils when the call came. Hugh answered before she could dry her hands and cross the room.

"Mom!" he yelled from the den. "It's for you. Some doctor."

"Thanks, Hugh, I have it." She held the receiver a moment, then put it to her ear. "Dr. Heller?"

"Yes. I hope I'm not interrupting your dinner."

"No, we've finished."

"I wonder—could you meet me? It's. . .well, it would be easier if I could see you. It won't take long. I'm at the hospital now. I could meet you at the Princeton Inn—if you can get away for a few minutes?"

He sounded upset. Maybe she really did have a brain tumor, and he wanted to break it to her face to face. Oh, that was absurd. "I guess so. Angelica's not here. I'll have to ask my neighbor to keep an eye on the boys—I won't be able to stay long."

"Of course, I understand. In the coffee shop in half an hour?"

"All right. I'll be there."

He was waiting when she arrived, his suit dark, his expression serious.

They spoke politely until their coffee was served. Later Liz couldn't remember what they'd talked about, probably the weather or something equally bland. After the waitress had set mugs of coffee in front of them and left, Liz waited, her eyes level with his, for what it was he wanted to say.

He ran a forefinger around the rim of his cup. Even cleared his throat. Good heavens, she thought.

"This is awkward for you—it is for me, too. I apologize for that. I've never discharged a patient before." He met her gaze. "I think it's best if you see another doctor. That's why I introduced you to Sam. He's an excellent physician, so I know you're in good hands. Of course, you're certainly welcome to find someone different, I just thought. . .well, I know how good Sam is." He looked away, his breathing shallow and rapid as though he'd run up a long flight of stairs.

Liz tried to make sense of what he was saying. "I don't understand. You think he's a better physician—for me—than you?"

He tapped the tines of the fork that lay unused on his napkin. "No, not necessarily, but. . .I can't have you as a patient." He raised his eyes to meet hers. They were a warm brown, and he used them in a way that had always fascinated her, imperceptibly narrowing and widening them as he spoke.

She waited, not asking the obvious question.

"You see. . .my interest in you is. . .it's grown to be. . .it's more than. . . ." He trailed off, his expression close to frantic. ". . .more than that of a doctor for his patient," he managed to finish.

At a complete loss, there was nothing she could think to say. She continued to look at him.

"I'd like to see you. . .socially." He added hastily, "I realize you may be involved in a relationship—you're a handsome woman," and he attempted a smile. "But I have to ask if that might be a possibility."

It took her a moment to realize that he was waiting for an answer. Her feelings were whirling away from her. She had come to the inn feeling hurt, and now she was feeling what almost amounted to tenderness for him, as he sat so vulnerable in his waiting.

She cleared her throat. "I don't know quite how to explain." She spread her hands in a gesture of confusion. "You see, I was married to Bo Donnely for fifteen years, and I. . .I still feel like his wife." She thought about his words and then said them aloud, "'Involved in a relationship.' So strange." She looked away, then down at the table, at his hands and noticed the gold wedding band.

He followed her gaze. "Separated," he said. "For a long time."

"You live in Aspenhill, and she. . .?"

"She lives in Connecticut."

She nodded. "I see. It must be lonely with your family gone."

He looked at her for a long moment, then said, "It is. I have a son, but he lives with my parents most of the time."

"Oh. Not too far away, I hope."

"In Queens. It works out well, actually. Will needs a special school, and there's an excellent one close to them."

They were quiet for a time. Then Liz fumbled for her sweater. "Don't leave."

Just the two words, but they carried with them a need that she didn't want to be responsible for filling. "I should get back. I don't know what to tell you, other than I'm flattered. I haven't been called an attractive woman in. . .well, I don't know how long. So thank you for that." She wished she knew how to exit gracefully.

"I didn't, you know. Call you an attractive woman."

Once again she found herself confused.

"Handsome. I said you were a handsome woman." He looked dead serious.

She grinned, relieved at the sudden absence of strain in the conversation. "You won't settle for a synonym?"

An answering grin lit up his face. "Okay, but just this once."

Pulling her sweater over her shoulders, she noticed the time on her watch. "I really do have to get back," she said.

"Give it a trial run."

"Pardon me?"

"One dinner. Can't hurt. And if you have a terrible time, I'll back off. You have my word."

"Well. . . ."

"Good. Tomorrow night?"

"Tomorrow night," she found herself repeating.

3

DINNER

SAM KAUFMAN PAUSED IN THE DOORWAY to Steve Heller's office, a hand up to his eyes to shade them from the early morning sun that was slanting through the slats of the window blind. "So, Steve, how'd it go yesterday?"

"How'd what go?"

"Come on. You know what I'm talking about. The Elizabeth Donnely meeting."

Steve shrugged and continued to study a page of test results from the lab. "Not so good."

"Hey, I'm sorry." Sam came into the room and folded himself into a chair next to the desk. "Did you meet her? Come on, what happened?"

Steve looked up, taking in his partner's strained eyes and poorly shaved face. "You don't look so great."

"Yeah, I was on call last night, and when it's my night, the phone never stops ringing. Seriously, she won't see you?"

"Tonight, but I don't think it's going anywhere." He put down the sheaf of papers. "Seems she's still in love with her husband."

"Who's dead."

"Yeah, we know that." He pulled open a drawer in the desk, took out a small plastic vial, and handed it to Sam. "Here. Put some of these drops in your eyes. They make mine feel gritty just looking at them. It doesn't mean you stop loving someone, just because he's dead—or in some cases, as good as dead."

Sam looked at him. "Yeah. Elisa."

"Sorry. I'm indulging in an orgy of self-pity. But she's a really nice person, and she's—"

"She's the first woman you've shown any interest in since Elisa," Sam said, cutting him off. He pushed himself out of the chair. "Look, you can't give up. Have a great time tonight, and who knows? Maybe she'll change her mind once she knows you."

Steve made a sound of disbelief. "Yeah."

That evening the young woman he had glimpsed in the doorway the night of Katie's death answered his ring. Short and stocky with gleaming black hair pulled back and tied with a bright orange ribbon, she had eyes as dark as her hair, set deep above high cheekbones that spoke of an Indian heritage. She wore a serious expression, as though the greeting of guests was not a matter to be taken lightly.

"Please to come in," she said over the din of barking and music. He stepped into a wide foyer, where he was met by two dogs, one small, one huge. "Mrs. Donnely, she expects you. You will wait here?" She indicated a wide door into a living room to his right. "Please, sit," she said, gesturing toward a wing chair, then left him to be thoroughly sniffed and disappeared down the hall.

He didn't recognize the breed of the small dog, which resembled a wiry-coated hound with short legs and a tail held high and waving, but the giant was a German shepherd with a regal ruff of buff colored fur. The shepherd apparently approved of him, for he began to lick Steve's hands while nudging his knee with his large and very solid head.

Over the distant beat of heavy metal music, he heard Elizabeth and a child conversing but couldn't make out what was being discussed. He looked around the room, which ran the depth of the house. The walls were painted a warm peach, the woodwork creamy white. It was a cheerful room, the windows tall and gently curtained, the chairs and sofas deep and welcoming. A vase filled with nodding blooms of white peonies filled the fireplace. The far end of the room was occupied by a baby grand piano, its rack filled with open music books. He walked over and glanced at the books, which contained both classical and jazz pieces, before turning his attention to the photographs on the mantel above the fireplace. The one on the far right was a studio portrait of Bo Donnely. Steve had only seen the senator once, over four years before—and before Elizabeth had become a patient. That was in the auditorium of Port Smith Hospital, where Donnely had sat on the hospital board of directors. He had been speaking to the medical staff about a bill on aid for prescription drugs for senior citizens. Steve had gotten held up and arrived late. He'd been directed to an empty seat on the side aisle near the front of the hall. A young woman sitting in the next seat had been looking out the window to her left, instead of at the speaker, prompting Steve, once he was seated, to lean over and whisper, "Pretty boring, huh?" and she had replied with a guilty smile.

Donnely had ended his speech by thanking various people including his wife, whom he asked to stand. The woman next to him had stood. Steve remembered that he'd had the grace to apologize to her during the final round of applause.

He ran his fingers along the silver frame, studying Bo Donnely's chiseled features, intense eyes, and the firm set to his mouth. His thick, prematurely gray hair had been expertly barbered to look charmingly unkempt—a handsome man, known during his run for Congress for that most desirable attribute in a politician, charisma—

"Give me that, you son of a *bitch!*"

The shout rang through the house, even managing to rise above the pounding decibels of music. The sound of thumping footsteps on a flight of stairs was accompanied by a child's drawn out wail of, "*Momm!*"

"Hugh." Elizabeth's voice. "Turn off that music." Silence. "No more," she called. "I won't have that language."

"Mom, that little bastard—"

"That's *it*, Hugh," she said, cutting him off. "Stay in your room the rest of the night. And no stereo." She had barely raised her voice, but it commanded attention. He recalled that she was a teacher.

Steve turned back to the mantel. The middle photograph was of two little boys on a beach, knee deep in a wave, their backs to the sea. The younger child, who had been to his office with Elizabeth, had a sturdy build, a mop of nearly white hair, and a sweet, trusting expression; the older, probably the profane Hugh, had his mother's features and a mischievous grin.

It was painful to look at the photograph on the left. Elizabeth holding Katie: identical curly, honey blonde hair, and eyes the luminous blue of an early summer sky; they faced one another, Katie's small, chubby hands clutching her mother's shoulders, their heads tipped back, their laughter almost audible. He turned away.

She came in then, Hugh's mischievous grin flirting at the corners of her mouth, and his breath quickened.

"It's not too late to bow out, you know," she said.

He smiled. "I was wondering if you'd rehearsed them."

She laughed. "I'm afraid I'm not that creative. I see you've met Mick and Bizzie."

The dogs lay in front of the fireplace, their eyes on Elizabeth, their tails thumping the carpet with a slow beat.

"Yes, I've been thoroughly examined and, I think, approved. Which is which?"

"This is Mickey," she said, going over to the dogs and kneeling to pet the smaller of the pair. "Biz is short for Bismark. He was Bo's dog." At the sound of Bo's name, the shepherd lifted his head and looked at the door.

"He still waits." Without turning her head, she said, "Harry, would you like to come in and say good evening to Dr. Heller?"

Steve looked over and saw the younger of the two boys standing in the doorway.

"Yes. I would."

"Come in then. You may not remember, but you met Dr. Heller last summer. You and Katie and I visited him in his office."

Harry moved further into the room, where he leaned against an end table and studied Steve. "I remember. There was a lady with hiccups there, and I told her she should hold her breath."

Elizabeth smiled. "That's right. I'd forgotten that."

"Do you remember her?" he asked Steve. "Did you cure her hiccups?"

"It was a tough case, Harry. I did get rid of them, but they came back."

"You should have sent her to another doctor."

Steve glanced at Elizabeth. "You're right, it would have been the wise thing to do."

"We're going to leave now, so you be good for Angelica." She bent and kissed him.

"Where're you going to eat? MacDonald's?"

"Oh, I don't know about that. It will be up to Dr. Heller."

"Are you? Going to MacDonald's?" He looked up at Steve.

"I'm not sure, but you know, if we don't eat dinner there, we'll probably stop for a milkshake on the way home." He paused for a beat, then said, "As long as we're there, we could probably get you a shake. That is, if you'd like one."

"Oh, yeah!" Harry's face lit up. "And Hugh and Angelica, too?"

"Definitely. Hugh and Angelica, too. What flavor do you like?"

"Vanilla and chocolate for Hugh and, wait, I have to ask Angelica." He sped off.

Steve looked at Elizabeth with raised eyebrows. "It's okay?"

She nodded.

"That's a good guy, thinking of the brother who just cursed him out."

"He's a very good guy."

Steve's choice of a restaurant did not, as Liz pointed out, resemble MacDonald's in any way. After they had ordered, he said, "I think it's vital to the success of this dinner that we drop the Dr. Heller and Mrs. Donnely. Are you okay with that?"

"All right. It's Steven H. Heller, isn't it? What does the 'H' stand for?"

He looked pained. "You don't want to know. Steve is fine."

"May I call you Steven? I like it better than Steve, if that's okay."

"That's okay. And you? Elizabeth?"

"Yes, or Liz."

He gazed at her intently, finally shaking his head. "I don't think so."

"You don't think so?"

"You're really not a Liz. I'm surprised no one's ever told you that."

"Then I suppose it's Elizabeth."

"A beautiful name, but. . .who were you named for?"

She raised her eyebrows. "My great aunt. I've always been happy to have her name," she said, somewhat defensively.

"And she was called Elizabeth?"

She looked thoughtful. "No, she was called Lizzie."

"Lizzie."

"Lizzie? You've got to be kidding. It sounds like an old car—or an ax murderer. You want to call me Lizzie?"

"Yes, I do." He watched her face as she thought about the unfamiliar name. She had fine, patrician features with the exception of her mouth, which was wide, the upper lip well-defined, the lower one generous. A senusal mouth.

"All right, I guess. Call me Lizzie, if it makes you happy."

"It makes me happy. And with Mrs. Donnely and Dr. Heller out of the way, we can order."

Dinner was a long affair. Steve loved to watch her face as she talked, loved her voice, the way she made small, graceful gestures with her hands.

They discussed her job teaching a group of learning disabled boys at a small private school in Port Smith. He told her about his son's congenital hearing loss and his struggle with learning. She shared with him her on-going battle with Hugh and his unacceptable vocabulary. They were easy with one another, no awkward pauses, no stilted questions.

They remembered to stop for milkshakes. Driving back to Stelfox Street, Steve tapped the clock on the dash. "I'm afraid it's late for Harry to be awake. Think he's waiting for his milkshake?"

"If not, he'll get up when we arrive with them. It's okay. It'll be a special night for him, and special occasions make for good memories."

"And yours? Your memory of tonight?"

Out of the corner of his eye he saw her glance at him. "I had a really nice time, Steven. It will be a lovely memory."

He braked for a light. "That sounds past tense. Maybe I shouldn't have couched the question in terms of memory."

"I. . .I don't know what to say. I guess because I don't know where you're going with this. I don't want to. . . what? I guess I don't want you to have expectations. . . that I can't fill."

They drove in silence for a few minutes.

"I don't have any expectations." He pulled into her driveway, put the car in park, and turned to her. "My friends all seem to be couples, which I find either awkward or lonely. I know you said you still feel like a married woman." He reached into the back seat for the MacDonald's bag. "Bo's been dead nearly two years," he said as gently as he could.

She nodded. "I know. And you're right. It can be lonely when your friends are all married. But. . . ."

"No demands. An occasional dinner, a movie. . .I enjoy your company and. . .perhaps you enjoy mine."

She didn't respond. He turned and opened the door. "Let's get these to the boys while they're still cold. Lizzie, give my idea some thought."

4

ANGELICA

WHEN STEVE THOUGHT OF LIZZIE, which was often during the long month of May, he had to stop, or he found himself caught in the kind of bleakness he hadn't felt since Elisa left for Connecticut that last and final time. For Lizzie was side-stepping his several invitations, and he was increasingly convinced that a future relationship wasn't going to happen. While he hated the image of himself as pitiful beggar, he couldn't stamp out the shoot of hope he secretly nursed.

And so he found himself dialing her number late on a Thursday afternoon, with Memorial Day weekend looming.

"I don't know, Steven, this is proving to be a long week. At school I have a class of eight emotionally fragile boys who are unable to learn, let alone sit still, because their hormones are raging, and they've had it up to the tips of their spiked hair with education. And at home I have two boys who are experts at pushing each other's buttons. By tomorrow night I may not be fit company."

"It might be a draw—I've been seeing patients with allergies all week. Believe me, there's no one crankier than someone whose eyes itch, nose runs, and throat's raw. A doctor's life isn't as safe as you probably imagine."

Lizzie laughed. "Okay, you just might win the prize in the worn-out professional category. Look—how about we eat here? You could pick up a movie, if you like."

"Are you sure? I mean about fixing dinner." He tried to damp down the surprise and eagerness in his voice. "Because I can pick up food as well as a movie."

"No, no. You don't get out of eating my cooking that easy. But if you do bring a movie, I need to warn you that I don't do those 'twenty-five-hundred get gunned down in the first three minutes' kind of films that you guys seem to love."

"Oh, right. *Bambi* or nothing, huh?"

"Well, maybe *The Wizard of Oz*, but I don't know. That witch stuff is pretty creepy."

"Okay, I think I'm getting the picture. What time?"

"What time do you usually head home on a Friday night?"

"Six-thirty, seven."

"That's fine. Hugh and Harry will have eaten by then."

Angelica, Biz, and Mickey answered the door when Steve arrived.

"Please to come in, Dr. Heller," Angelica said. Her dark eyes regarded him gravely, her canary yellow sweater a study in contrast to her dour expression. She held the door wide with one hand, while the other kept a firm grip on Biz's collar.

"Good evening, Angelica. How are the dogs this evening?"

"They are so happy to be seeing you. Dr. Heller, you will see these photographs of Senator Bo Donnely?" She beckoned him to the bookshelves that lined the wall opposite the staircase. There were numerous photographs of the senator: Bo with the governor, Bo and Lizzie being greeted by a child bearing a bouquet of flowers, Bo in the state house with colleagues, Bo with the New Jersey Devils hockey team, and a lot more.

Angelica ran reverent fingers over a frame.

"Very impressive, Angelica. Thanks for showing them to me." He picked up one that showed Bo, Lizzie, and the children with the Statue of Liberty in the background. Bo was standing with a hand on each of his boys' shoulders. All three were dressed in dark blazers, light-colored slacks, and red, white, and blue ties. Lizzie, her dress and hair blowing in the wind, stood to the side holding an infant Katie. The photographer had caught them in a serious moment. None of them was smiling.

"And here, Doctor, is *Time* magazine. You will see Senator Donnely is on the cover." Angelica displayed a framed copy of the magazine, her face now aglow.

Steve remembered that particular issue. It had run in the spring before Bo's death in July. He shared the cover with several men and women who were strong candidates for the House of Representatives in the November elections that year.

"Hey." A boy came into the foyer.

"Hello," Steve said. "You must be Hugh."

He nodded. "Nice to meet you, Dr. Heller." Hugh shook Steve's hand, his eyes intently studying Steve's face. Tall, with abundant auburn hair and freckles across his cheekbones and nose, the boy's resemblance to Lizzie—with the exception of his coloring—was strong. He stood bouncing on the toes of his sneakers for a moment, then said, "Mom says I'm to apologize for swearing the other week when you were here." He shoved his hands into the back pockets of his jeans. "I guess I'm sorry, but sometimes Harry drives me nuts. And he gets away with goddamn—"

"Hugh," Angelica warned.

"Okay, okay. Sorry." Turning to her, he said, "Angelica, I can't find my NFL sweatshirt. It isn't where I left it," he said hesitantly, looking down and watching his toe draw a circle on the carpet. "You know where it is?"

"Yes, Hugh. Where it is you left it?"

"I know, I know, I didn't put it away, and you had to pick it up. Honest to God, Angelica, next time I will. I'll fold it and I'll put it in a drawer. I'll start all over, being neat, you'll see. But please, can I have it this one time?"

"Dr. Heller, you should guess how many times it is Hugh has started over."

"Well, let's see. Maybe two or three times?"

"It is more like two or three *hundred!* Such a boy. Hugh, you come now, and I show you where you need to put the shirt. . . . You will excuse, please, Doctor? Mrs. Donnely, she is in the kitchen. She said you go there."

He continued down the hall and turning left, found the kitchen. Lizzie was at the stove, stirring a pot, sending waves of a spicy aroma through the air. Pausing in the doorway, he glanced around the warm, steamy room and couldn't help compare its butcher block and tile surfaces, its hanging plants and crowded bulletin board with the sterile white and chrome expanses of his own kitchen.

"Hey, there you are." She wore a butcher's apron over jeans and a long-sleeve black tee shirt. A red figured scarf covered her hair. She looked, Steve thought, just right for a Friday evening at home. When she turned to him, he noticed again how startling blue her eyes were—and, more important, how free of neediness. He'd had enough of neediness to last him a lifetime.

Noting his offerings, she said, "Oh, how thoughtful, you brought wine. I have a bottle chilling. Let's save this for another time, okay?"

Another time, he repeated silently. Two great words. "Sounds good to me. And how's *Erin Brocovitch* for a movie? They assured me there's no on-screen violence. Have you seen it?"

"Perfect choice. No, I never get to the movies. Well, that's not true. Once in awhile I take Harry and his pals. You know, the Dalmations, the Hulk, all those good ones."

He laughed. "I've seen a couple of those myself."

Over dinner he mentioned the photographs.

"Ah. I see Angelica gave you the tour."

"Yeah, I was wondering—was she telling me something?"

"Telling you something? Oh, you mean like, 'This is Bo Donnely's house, you'd better get lost?'" She grinned. "No, Angelica gives that tour to all my friends, male and female. She adored Bo, you see. Actually, it was no secret—she was in love with him."

"Really. Wasn't that. . .uncomfortable?"

"For me?"

He nodded. "The housekeeper chasing after the master of the house?"

Lizzie shook her head. "No, I'm sorry, I should have explained about Angelica. She's not the housekeeper, she lives here. In the apartment above the garage."

"But. . .she answers the door."

Lizzie shrugged. "I answer the door when I'm free." She put her fork down. "Let me tell you how she got to be here. That will explain why she adored Bo.

"Angelica's from Guatemala. Her father and brothers, practically all the men in her family, were strongly involved with the antigovernment movement there. At one point, things got very unsafe for all the family members, the women as well as the men."

She handed him the napkin-covered bread basket.

"That's when Angelica's mother decided she had to get her daughters away from the fighting, to some place where they could lead normal lives. So she arranged for Angelica and her sister Edena to get to the United States." She looked at Steve's empty plate.

"Can I get you more? There's plenty, so please have more if you're hungry."

"I'm hungry, and I love it, but I don't know what it is."

"It is a little strange looking," she said. Returning with a full plate, she placed it in front of him. "It's a Moroccan recipe, cous cous with lamb and tomatoes and raisins and almonds."

"It's delicious." He held the wine bottle over her glass, but she shook her head. "Go on about Angelica. We left her on her way to the U.S."

"Yes, and she and Edena got here, but there was a hitch. No visas, no green cards. They asked for asylum, as they'd been instructed to do, but they were told they'd have to wait for their cases to be heard. Meanwhile, they got jobs in New Jersey—Angelica as a nanny for the children of an associate in Bo's law firm. When the INS decided to send the girls home, he—Paul Berman, the associate—went to Bo for help. After listening to him, Bo realized that the chances of Angelica not being arrested upon her return were nil. So he went to work, called in favors, did everything possible to get her another hearing."

"And it worked?"

"It did. The INS reversed themselves, and from then on Angelica believed the sun rose and set on Bo. I swear, if he'd asked her to jump off the GW Bridge, she would have done it without question."

"And she lives here. With you, I mean."

"Yes, Paul's kids had gotten old enough that they didn't need a nanny, and we did. So Angelica moved in and helped me with the kids. Now. . .well. . . ." She looked away for a moment, and Steve thought of Katie.

She cleared her throat. "Now Harry's in school all day, and Hugh is nine and practically self-sufficient, so I don't need a full-time nanny."

"Does she work?"

"Yes, she has a part-time job, and she still helps me. If she's here and I go out, she takes over. And she does a lot of the housework, since I've gone back to teaching."

"What happened to Edena?"

Lizzie shook her head and didn't answer for a minute. Finally, she said, "Not good. Bo had everything just about set so that she could remain, but the INS shipped her back before the hearing." She finished her wine. "Edena never made it through customs in

Guatemala. Her mother was notified a week later to come and get her body."

They sat for a few minutes, listening to the muffled voices on the television in the den.

Later, driving home, he was able to pinpoint the cause of the downward swoops in the roller coaster ride his emotions were taking—and that was Bo Donnely. Christ, the man had been intelligent, handsome, able to save a woman from a death squad, and had fought like hell to try to save another. What was not to admire. . .and love. . .and miss? He must be crazy to think he could take Bo's place in his widow's affections.

And yet, when the roller coaster was at its peak—he considered adjectives to describe his feelings and came up with "euphoric" and "elated"—it was like seeing color after years of a black and white existence.

5

GAME

JUNE, AND IT FELT LIKE THE DOG DAYS OF AUGUST. Liz wiped wet palms on her slacks before touching the steering wheel. She wondered if it was a waste of God's time to ask him for a parking spot in the shade?

It was four-fifteen. She had three—no, four errands to run before she could pick up Harry and get to Hugh's final baseball game of the season, due to begin at five o'clock. Holding the wheel gingerly, she eased into traffic, squinting, even with sunglasses, in the glare of sun on the hot metal of cars that jammed Broad Avenue.

The day before, Hugh had come home from the bank where he had a savings account to tell her that he'd seen her friend Dr. Heller.

At the stove stirring marinara sauce, she'd taken a moment,

scraping the side of the pot, before responding.

"That's nice. I hope you said hello."

"No, Mom, I ran the other way." She'd sent him a sharp look.

"Okay, sorry. Yes, I said hello. We talked. He knows a lot about baseball."

"Does he? And what about at the bank? Did you get your pass-book problem straightened out?"

"Yeah." He'd sighed. "They were right. As usual."

Liz had stifled a smile: Hugh was determined to catch the bank in an error.

"Don't go off on your bike, Hugh. We'll be eating soon."

He'd been half way out the door. "Okay, I'll be around. Oh, and Mom? I invited Dr. Heller to my game tomorrow."

His invitation had surprised her. Hugh rarely noticed—or seemed to care—whether even she and Harry made it to his games. He played exceptionally well, focusing all his attention on what was going on out on the field.

The other thing about the invitation was that she wished it hadn't been extended. She would never have said that to Hugh, but after two dinners she'd been hoping that Steven Heller would lose interest in seeing her. Not that she hadn't enjoyed their evenings together, because she had. And that was where it ended for her, but she was afraid it didn't end there for him. She had been troubled enough to talk to Annie West about it.

"What makes you uncomfortable?" Annie had asked.

"His intentions. I ask myself, what does he want? I don't know, the whole thing makes me. . .uncomfortable."

"The next time he calls, would it make sense to ask him what he wants out of the relationship?"

"But you see, you're calling it a relationship. Annie, I don't have the desire—or the time—to enter into a relationship with a man."

"With a friend?"

Liz had studied her for a moment. "That's how Steven described it. He likes my company." She tilted her head in thought. "Is that valid, do you think?"

Annie hadn't answered. Liz had sighed. "He seems honest. And sad—you know, separated from his wife and his son. I hate to play the villain."

Annie had smiled. "You never struck me as the villain type. What I'm hearing is sympathy—no, empathy—for another human being."

"Human being. That doesn't sound threatening. It's his maleness that scares me. Maybe I'm making trouble where none exists?"

"Could be."

And they had left it at that. Well, if he came to the game, she'd put the human being proposition to the test.

She found Harry hopping from one sneakered foot to the other in the driveway, his hair sticking together in clumps and dark with perspiration, his tee shirt rumpled, and his shorts sagging down his sturdy hips.

"Mom, where have you been? We're late. We'll miss the game!"

He was chattering non-stop before they reached Grand Avenue, a block away. "Harry," she interrupted, "did you remember to bring the permission slip home for me to sign?" Harry's class was going on a hike in Tallman Park on Friday, going at that point without Harry, who had forgotten the permission slip every day for the past week.

"Uh-huh, I got it. Will we get to climb, Mom?"

"Oh, I hope not, Harry."

"Aw, Mom, I can't keep climbing dumb old trees." He sank down in his seat. "They're just practice. I gotta try a mountain."

"Someday you will, sweetheart, when you're a little older. Scaling mountains is serious business." Harry was her climber, something she had been ill-prepared for. Hugh was cautious, preferring two feet on the ground at all times. When Harry came along, she'd watched him master ropes, jungle gyms, and trees with her heart doing flip-flops and her arms ready to catch him.

At the little league field the wooden bleachers were crowded with families and friends of both teams. As Liz and Harry approached them, he cried, "Mom, look, there's Dr. Heller! Hey, Dr.Heller!"

"Hey, Harry, I thought you missed the bus." Steve moved to his right to make room for them.

Harry laughed. "That's silly, we didn't come on a bus." He plunked down next to Steve and sat flush against him. "Is Hugh pitching?"

Steve smiled down at Harry. "He is, and you're just in time. See? He's walking out to the mound right now." He looked up at Liz, studied her for a moment, then asked, "How are you, Lizzie? You look a little frazzled. You okay?"

"I'm okay." Waving to several people as she sat down next to Harry, she shaded her eyes with one hand and turned her attention to the field. Orange and green caps bobbed up and down as the teams threw balls around. She located Hugh's orange cap on the pitcher's mound, where he was warming up. "I'm glad you came."

Steve gazed at her over Harry's tow head. "Why is that?"

She met his gaze. "For a couple of reasons."

"And they might be?"

"Well, one, you get to see what frazzled looks like."

He smiled. "Okay, it's not looking so bad. And two?"

"Two, Hugh will be happy you made it. Did you have to leave patients waiting in the examining rooms?"

"Oh, yeah, several."

It was Liz's turn to grin. She turned her attention back to the field, aware that she was being watched by more than one pair of curious eyes. Parents, all those mothers and fathers of Hugh's team members, would be speculating as to who Steven was.

Harry managed to sit still for an inning and a half, then scrambled down the stand to join boys he knew from school. Steve moved over.

"Could I take you and the boys to dinner later?"

"I promised Harry dinner at McDonald's. Hugh will eat with his team." She hesitated, then asked, "Are you up for a Big Mac?"

"Love a Big Mac."

"You'll probably need two by the time the game's over."

The Port Smith McDonald's was crowded and noisy, exactly the way Harry liked his dining spots.

"What did you say?" Liz asked, leaning across the table to improve her chances of hearing Steven.

"I said, 'Would you be interested in attending a cocktail party Saturday evening?' I'll add, just so you know up front, it will be mostly doctors."

"Doctors don't scare me. I guess so. Is there a catch? You don't sound as though you're dying to go."

He made a face. "Cocktail parties aren't my favorite thing, but I need to go to this one. There's someone from Mass General I want to meet, and he's supposed to be there."

"Look! Hugh's team is here!" Harry twisted around in order to see over the back of the booth.

Liz waved to Hugh. "I see them, the district champs."

"Yeah. Hugh'll probably eat double fries and at least two Big Macs." Harry looked wistful.

"That's how a champ eats, Harry," Steve commiserated.

6

COCKTAILS

A<small>LTHOUGH</small> M<small>ICKEY AND</small> B<small>IZ CLAMORED</small> for his attention, Steve gave it all to Lizzie, who had hesitated partway down the steps from the second floor, a frown of indecision on her face. "Too dressy?" she wondered aloud.

He shook his head, which was on a level with her feet in barely there, high-heeled sandals. "No. You look beautiful."

Her cheeks flushed. "I wasn't looking for compliments. . .really."

He continued to gaze at her as she came down the last few steps. She was stunning in a white linen dress that fell in tiers from spaghetti straps and ended just at her knees. Her hair was held back from her forehead, the curls around her face tamed by intricate twists and glistening with a wet gel.

"Yes?" Eyebrows raised, she questioned his stare.

"Sorry." He grinned. "But you usually don't reveal your legs."

"Umm. I take it from your leer that they pass muster." She eyed him up and down. "You look pretty sharp yourself, Doc, but. . .no shorts? Because I've never seen *your* legs."

He laughed. "Fair enough. No, physicians wear long pants, which is how you can distinguish us from surgeons. Who *do* wear shorts."

She smiled, and the way it lit her face caused serious upheavals in his chest. "Let me check on the boys, and I'll be ready," she said.

"This affair's at the Medfords'," Steve said as they drove along a winding road in the East Hill section of Port Smith. "Do you know them?"

"He's chairman of the hospital board, isn't he?"

"He is, and his brother-in-law is Charles Callaway from Mass General. He heads the department of gerontology at Harvard."

"I see. Is it okay to ask why you want to meet him?"

"Sure. Callaway's in the process of setting up a large-scale longitudinal study, and Sam and I hope to convince him that Port Smith should be one of the study sites. We figure it won't hurt to have Dick Medford introduce us."

"The study has to do with aging?"

"It's going to look at medication strengths for people over seventy."

"I see. Won't it entail a great deal of work for you and Dr. Kaufman? I mean, in addition to your practice—or would you give that up?"

"No," he said quickly. "I'd never do that," he added, then

smiled. "Guess we'll just have to create more hours in the day."

"Right, that'll work." She watched the road for a few minutes. "You love what you do." It was a statement, not a question. "Bo did, too," she continued quietly. "Being a lawyer was okay, but when he went into politics, he. . . well, he loved every aspect of it."

He glanced at her, but she had turned her head to look out the side window. She rarely spoke of Bo, and, while he thought he should respond, he knew from her body language that the subject was closed.

The party was being held on the terraces and in the gardens of Anita and Richard Medford, who had chosen the perfect Saturday evening in June for their annual affair for the hospital medical staff. The temperature hovered just below eighty, the breeze was laden with the scents of lavender and roses, and the late summer evening sunlight, slanting through towering oaks and pines, bathed greenery and guests alike.

They left the car to a young man with the valet parking service and strolled across the grass to a side terrace where the Medfords were greeting their guests.

"Elizabeth, wonderful to see you," Richard Medford greeted her, taking her hand and lightly kissing her cheek. "How are you, my dear? Are you getting on all right? A terrible loss, your husband, a loss not only for New Jersey but for the nation. What a congressman he would have made."

Giving her hand a final squeeze, he turned to Steve. "Heller, isn't it?"

Steve introduced himself and mentioned that he had heard Dr. Callaway was visiting.

"You know Charles?"

"I don't, but I'm hoping you'll introduce us. I read his recent article in the *New England Journal*, and, of course, both of his books."

"Excellent. Let me take you over to meet him, and, Anita, perhaps you'll see that Elizabeth gets a drink."

Anita flagged a waiter, who hurried off to get Liz a glass of white wine, before introducing her to several people and showing her the water garden.

"Anita, who is this lovely person? Surely she has nothing to do with the medical profession."

The women turned to the tall blond man who had approached them.

"You're right, no connection—other than being accompanied by Steve Heller," Anita added. "Elizabeth Donnely, Dan Taylor. Would you excuse me, my dears? I see some new arrivals I should greet."

"Elizabeth. One of my favorite names, it invokes the regal—yet brims with great warmth." He bent toward her, a dreamy smile hovering on his lips.

"Dan Taylor. I take it you do have a connection to the medical profession."

"Guilty. Dermatology, I'm afraid, although, if one must be in this business, it's the only specialty to have. Can I get you something to drink?"

"No, here's my wine now." She smiled her thanks to the waiter and took the proffered glass.

"Let me recall—what does Steve practice?" He squinted, pretending deep thought. "Internal medicine, right? Oh, yes, he and that partner of his are working up to a grand study. Makes you wonder how he has time for a party. Rumor has it that he's putting in long hours trying to secure Port Smith for this thing on aging." He shuddered. "Aging—so depressing. Can you imagine?"

Not waiting for an answer, he took her by the elbow. "Please, let me show you the rose gardens. We must find the perfect shade of pink to enhance your fabulous complexion. New Dawn, perhaps, one of my favorite roses."

Across the terrace Steve joined Sam Kaufman and his wife Wendy, who was Sam's opposite in appearance. Short with dark hair and eyes, she possessed the physical energy of a cheerleader.

"Hey, I think the hospital's own Don Juan is hitting on your date," she said, nodding toward Liz. "Don't you think you guys should rescue her?"

"Yeah, I'm going to, that is if she wants rescuing," Steve said.

They watched as Taylor guided a smiling Liz across the lawn. "But first, how'd you get on with Callaway, Sam? I just spoke to him, and I think he seemed interested. At least he didn't cut me off."

Wendy sighed. "Can't we enjoy the evening and the fact that neither of you is on call—and forget the study?"

Steve gave her a quick hug. "Three minutes, that's all I ask. After that, the evening is yours to enjoy. I promise," he added when she looked unconvinced.

When they had finished, Sam said, "We're going for dinner when we leave here. Why don't you and Elizabeth join us?"

"Sounds good. I'll ask her and get back to you."

Liz joined him at the edge of the terrace, holding a rose. "That's lovely."

She brought the blush pink flower to her lips. "Perfect for my fabulous complexion. I have it on good authority." She kept a straight face, but the laugh lines at the corners of her eyes crinkled.

"Dr. Dan?"

"How'd you guess?"

He smiled at her and wondered how long he could stand this "just friends" situation.

7

SHOPPING

"You've worn that suit every day this week." Sam Kaufman looked at his partner and shook his head in mock disgust. "You have to go shopping, Steve, or patients will think our practice is failing. And, believe me, when that happens they flee like rats from a sinking ship."

"I happen to be very fond of this suit." Steve adjusted the film he was studying in the light box. "And don't compare our patients to rats. They'll take offense."

"Seriously, when did you last go clothes shopping?"

Steve frowned. "Let's see. . .1999? Or maybe it was '98."

Sam's eyes widened. "For Pete's sake, go spend some money on yourself. Take your friend Elizabeth with you. You can go tomorrow, it's your Saturday off."

"Shopping? I don't know. What do you think, Carrie?"

Carrie Jackson, a nurse who had been with the practice since its inception, was passing them in the hall.

"About what, Dr. Heller?"

"My suit. Sam thinks it's scaring patients away."

The corners of Carrie's thin lips almost succeeded in making it to a smile before she took charge and set them into their usual straight, stern line. She looked at the suit in question—a slightly rumpled, tan, single-breasted affair—and in a drill sergeant's voice that belied the affection in her eyes, said, "Get rid of that suit, by all means. We're sick of seeing it." She continued down the hall, calling over her shoulder, "And get some new ties while you're at it."

Steve removed the film and switched off the light box. "That's what's great about working around here. Everyone's so diplomatic."

But he called Lizzie that evening, because shopping had reminded him that he needed to buy something for Will's birthday, which was the following week. So far, it seemed Lizzie Donnely had thwarted his intentions at every turn. The night of the cocktail party at the Medfords' in June, she had told him that she and the boys always spent most of their summer in Nantucket. He had called her once they'd returned, but she'd pleaded a busy schedule when he suggested getting together.

"The mall? Tomorrow?" The line hummed for a few moments before she said, "Tomorrow might be a good day for me to go to the mall."

She was sitting on the porch when he pulled into the driveway. Tan, her hair streaked several shades lighter from the Nantucket sun, she appeared eager to set out on their excursion. Shopping, he thought. He would have to remember that the next time he had trouble pinning her down for a date.

"So what are we shopping for?" she asked him as he drove slowly past parked cars, looking for a space.

"A birthday present for Will. He'll be six next week, about Harry's age. I never know what to get him, and I figured you'd be a good resource."

"Toy shopping—an area I excel in. Don't worry, we'll find Will a great gift."

They were drawn into FAO Schwartz on a tide of children's excited voices. Not a tall man, Steve felt like one as Lizzie and he made their way into the store, side-stepping short bodies power-balling up and down aisles lined with the magic of a kid's Oz.

A salesman who spotted them and bustled over seemed eager to assist them in their search. "How old did you say the little boy is, Mr.—"

"Heller," Steve said. "Six. He's having his sixth birthday."

"Excellent. And what about special interests? Perhaps sports? Or science?"

"Let me think," Steve said. "Nature, maybe—or animals?"

"Ah, I may have just the thing. Let me see if it's on display. It will only take me a moment."

Steve turned to Lizzie, who was holding a large and benign looking stuffed gorilla. "Other than this guy," he said, indicating the gorilla, "do you see anything to capture the heart of a six year-old?"

"There was a remote-control car we passed on our way in. Wait here for Mr. Ames, and I'll go and give it a closer look."

Steve raised an eyebrow. "Mr. Ames?"

"The nametag on his lapel. You have to pay attention when you're shopping, Steven. Salespeople like to be called by name." She winked as she gave his arm a pat and headed for the front of the store.

When Ames returned with an insect identifying kit and an ant farm, Steve excused himself and went to find Lizzie to get her opinion. He was sure his mother wouldn't welcome an ant farm, but Lizzie might have a better take on that than he did. When he found her up front, he saw immediately that something was wrong. She was standing, the stuffed gorilla on the floor at her feet, staring at the entrance, her face drained of color. He followed her gaze and drew a sharp breath.

Entering the store and approaching Lizzie was a woman with a little girl. The child's eyes were wide at the sight of the toy wonderland, her blond curls forming a shining frame to her sweet expression. She was Katie Donnely's double. Steve reached Lizzie as her hands sought the support of the counter and, putting his arm around her shoulders, he steered her past the child toward the doors to the mall, shaking his head at Ames, who was following them.

In the doorway she stopped. "No, Steven, I have to—"

"We're leaving," he said.

Out in the mall she stopped again, her breathing ragged. "Please. . .I shouldn't fall apart. . .I just. . .can't let myself do this." He could feel the tremors running through her.

"Lizzie, listen to me. There are times to be strong, and there are times to retreat. . .to allow yourself to grieve. Today we're retreating. Come on." He started walking, guiding her along. "We need a drink."

The restaurant was packed with Saturday shoppers taking a break for lunch, the noise level edging toward intolerable.

Steve put aside the menus. "What will you have?"

"I can't."

"You can't? Why can't you?"

"You'd have to carry me out."

"I can do that."

"Maybe. . .maybe a glass of wine."

"No. No, this isn't a wine situation." Turning to the waiter who had appeared, he said, "She'll have a gin and tonic, and bring me a Scotch and water."

He was surprised at the speed with which she made the gin and tonic disappear. He ordered her another, but, of course, she had been right. She couldn't drink. He ended up helping her back to the car.

"You better drive," she said.

"Okay."

"Where did I park my car?"

"We came in my car, remember? And I think I parked it right over there." He nodded toward a black Audi.

"Didn't I drive here? I'm sure I drove here. I always drive to the mall."

The traffic leaving the mall was heavy, and they could only inch toward Route 4. She started to cry as they reached the top of the ramp and merged into the right lane of the highway—terrible, wrenching sobs that made him want to hit someone. How could a righteous god tear that beautiful child from her? He took the first exit and found a place to pull over.

He held her. Between sobs, she gasped, "Today. . . it's. . .today is her birthday. She'll. . .she would have been three."

"Oh, Christ. Lizzie, I'm so sorry." He found his handkerchief and wiped her face. "I'm so sorry," was all he could think to say.

When her sobs subsided, he released her, tucking the handkerchief into her hand, and started home again. Stopped at a light, he looked at her. She leaned over and kissed him, her lips damp and soft and salty on his mouth. He stifled the groan that tore through him. The car behind honked, and he drove on.

When next he looked, she was asleep.

She didn't waken until he stopped the car in her driveway.

"Sorry, Steven."

"Don't, Lizzie. Don't say that."

"I can manage." She opened the door and got out. Leaning back in, she said, "Sometimes I think the grieving will never end. But you're right—it has to be."

8

OPERA

WHILE THE TRI-STATE AREA WEATHER FORECASTERS couldn't agree on the timing or severity, they were of one accord on the path of a weakened, but still threatening Hurricane Flora, and northern New Jersey lay directly in it. Steve loaded Will into the car, drove him back to Queens earlier than usual, and, turning down his mother's invitation for dinner, joined the thick, crawling, Jersey-bound traffic across the bridge. Overhead black clouds, swept along by a quickening wind, filled a low, gray sky. Beneath him the Hudson, roiled by the same wind, tossed in sea-sick fashion the few small boats brave or foolhardy enough to have ventured out. Once back in Aspenhill, he took a left on Stelfox Street. He knew Lizzie was a capable and resourceful woman, perfectly able to handle a storm, but still. . .

The front door was open, and through the screen came the impassioned voice of Tosca pleading for. . .he forgot what Tosca pleaded for, her life probably. Either the bell wasn't working, or Tosca's strong soprano voice was too much for it, so he shushed the dogs and let himself in.

The boys voices, caught up in the ritual of brotherly bickering, came from the den. He found them stretched out on the floor with Battleship game boards. Their greetings were subdued and their expressions wary. The room, lamp-lit in the approaching dusk, smelled of apples and cinnamon and little boys.

"Everything okay?" he asked. "The radio says we're going to get a storm tonight."

"Yeah, a hurricane," Harry said.

Both of them were watching him closely.

Hugh finally spoke. "Mom's listening to opera."

"I hear that."

"You like opera, Steve?"

"Not a whole lot. Probably because I don't understand it."

They nodded, but continued to monitor him. "Are you going to turn it off?" Hugh asked.

"Off? No." He sat down on the edge of the couch. He was missing something, but he sure as hell didn't know what. "Your mom enjoys it, doesn't she?"

Hugh rattled game pieces in his hand. Harry chewed on the sleeve of his shirt. They didn't reply.

"Well. Guess you want to play your game. Who's winning?"

Hugh dropped his eyes and studied his gameboard. "My dad used to turn it off," he said.

"Turn it off? Oh, you mean the music."

They nodded.

"I see. He didn't like opera?"

Hugh and Harry exchanged glances.

"He hated it!" Harry crowed, flinging himself over into a sitting position and hugging his knees. "He said it sounded like dying ele-phants!"

"Dying elephants—that's a terrible sound. What about you guys, do you like it?"

They assured him they didn't. "But," Hugh allowed, "Mom lets me listen to my music, so. . ." He shrugged.

Steve got up. "Okay. I think I'll go in and say hello to her. You'll want to get on with your game."

He felt their eyes follow him as he walked toward the kitchen.

9

METS

"Get the popcorn, Mom, hurry, it's starting." Harry danced in nervous circles around the kitchen, jiggling the waiting bowl.

"Okay, okay, take it easy." Lizzie entered the time on the microwave. Odd that she was beginning to think of herself as Lizzie. Once in awhile she paused to ask herself what that meant, but most of the time she accepted it as a change she neither liked nor disliked. It simply was.

"Oh, no, I hear the singing! We're going to miss the first pitch."

"Almost ready. You go in—I'll put the popcorn in the bowl and be right there."

"We should have boxes, like at a real game."

"Hmm, I'll have to look into that."

★ ★ ★

To Lizzie and Harry's distress, the Mets were struggling by the bottom of the third. To make matters worse, they saw from the scores on the bottom of the screen that the Yankees were pummeling the Red Sox. They both hated it when the Mets lost and the Yankees won, knowing Hugh, an ardent Yankee fan, would be sure to mention it several hundred times in the next twenty-four hours.

When the doorbell rang, Mike Piazza was up with a full count and two outs. Harry and Lizzie couldn't tear themselves away to answer it.

It was Angelica who opened the door to Dr. Heller.

"Please to come in, Doctor. Mrs. Donnely, she is in the den with Harry. They watch their baseball. Shall I call her, or would you like?"

"I would like, Angelica. I don't want to interrupt the game." He rubbed the dogs' heads.

"Yes, she is very much the fan. She and Harry cheer the Mets, and Hugh cheers the Yankees. Sometimes very loud baseball arguments."

Steve followed the salty smell of popcorn to the den. "So how are the Yanks doing tonight?" he asked.

"Not the Yanks, Steve, the Mets! We hate the Yanks in this house."

"Harry," Lizzie warned.

"Okay, most of us don't like the Yanks."

Lizzie got up. "I can't bear to watch anymore. I'll get refreshments. Soda for Harry, coffee for Angelica and me. What would you like, Steven?"

"A beer if you have one. I'll get it, but first I'm going to watch Leiter strike this Phillie out."

"You know Al Leiter?" Harry asked, rolling onto his back and gazing up at Steve from his position on the floor in front of the TV set.

"Yes, I do. Not personally, you understand, but I like to watch him pitch."

In the kitchen he located a bottle of beer in the refrigerator and accepted the glass she handed him. "Let's take Harry to a game."

"Really?" She turned with the coffee carafe in her hands. "He'd love it. I would, too." She filled two mugs and put one on a tray along with a plate of cookies. "Let me take this to Angelica, and I'll be right back."

"I'm thinking," he said, when she returned, "that Will would probably enjoy a baseball game. We could pick him up on the way to Shea. What do you think?"

"Great, I think it's a great idea. I'd love to meet him."

"How about Hugh? Would he go?"

"I'm sure. He's a Yankee fan, but he loves any baseball, and he's only seen a couple major league games."

Two weeks later on a hot, sun drenched Saturday, Lizzie faced Steve on her front porch. "Steven, you're not really going to wear that, are you?"

"Are you referring to my polo shirt, my neatly pressed pants— or my Yankees cap?"

"You know I'm referring to the cap."

"Yep, I am, and I brought one for my buddy Hugh in case you hid his." He settled the cap he pulled from his back pocket onto Hugh's head, as he winked at Harry. "Nice cap, Harry. I've got an extra one like Hugh's and mine, if you want it."

"No way! Mom and I aren't going to get beat up. You wear those hats to Shea and they'll punch you, right, Mom?"

Steve looked at Lizzie. "I see she has a Mets cap." He continued to give her a quizzical look. "You've done something to your hair."

She put a hand to her head, pushing the cap back. "I braided it."

"I see that."

The car climbed the hill to the palisades. Lizzie fished a mirror out of her bag and looked into it. She had French braided her hair, no easy task. Usually worn in a bob cut somewhere between her ear and shoulder, it was thick and curly. There were lots of women who paid handsomely to have their hair permed to resemble hers, but she knew it only as a battleground, something to be tamed into presentable shape every morning. Now her head looked sleek and cool with the short, pinned up braids.

She felt Steve glancing over at her. "You think it looks weird."

"I think what looks weird?"

"You know, what you keep looking at—my hair."

"Did I say that?"

"You didn't say it in words, but your face says it."

He slowed to go through an EZ-Pass lane. "My face is lying. Your hair does not look weird."

She watched the car take the curve onto the approach to the George Washington Bridge.

"I can take them out. The braids, I mean."

"Lizzie, you're being silly. Your hair is fine."

Below them the Hudson sparkled in the mid-day autumn sunshine. "I think you hate it."

"I love your hair."

She swung to look at him, hearing an intensity in his voice that startled her, but he was leaning back, eyes on the car ahead of them, calling to the boys.

"Hey, fellas, look downstream at those boats. One's a police boat, and there's a police helicopter."

"Oh, cool! Look, Hugh!" Harry cried. "Probably there's a criminal in one of those boats."

"What do you know about criminals?" Hugh jeered. "You're only five."

"I know a lot. And, anyhow, I'm going to be six."

"Yeah, in half a year."

"Steve, how old is Willy?"

"He's six, Harry."

"Hey, like me, almost. Does he play baseball?"

"I think he'd like to play baseball, but he has some trouble running."

Harry pushed forward on the seat. "How come?"

"Will has a couple of problems." Steve checked the rear-view mirror. Harry's face was puzzled, Hugh's showed interest.

"Also, he doesn't hear as well as you or me, so he wears a hearing aid. It helps if he can see your face when you're talking to him."

"I know, so he can read your expression and your lips," Hugh said.

"Hugh's friend Jeanine has a hearing loss," Lizzie said.

"Can he sign?" Hugh asked.

"A little," Steve said.

"The Mets can sign," Harry said. "I'm going to watch them and learn."

"You are so clueless." Hugh sighed in disgust and put his ear phones on, opting out of any further conversation.

"Gramma, where are they? What if they forgot me?"

"Oh, sweetheart, you know your daddy would never forget you," Barbara Heller assured him as she adjusted his jeans and tucked a stray curl into his Yankees cap. "They'll be here soon. Did you go to the bathroom?"

"Yes. I told you a hundred times I did." He wriggled out of her reach and headed for the back door. "I'm going to get my baseball." Will's gait had a slight lurch to it, caused by his left foot dragging just enough to interfere with a smooth forward momentum.

Arthur Heller looked up from the newspaper he had been reading at the kitchen table. "I wish he'd get here, too. I'm hungry."

"We'll eat after they leave."

"I know. That's what I'm saying—the sooner he gets here, the sooner I can eat."

"I wish they'd eat here. I hope they at least come in. I'm curious to meet this friend of his."

"Friend?" Arthur looked over the top of his glasses at his wife, one eyebrow raised.

"That's what Steven said, that he was taking a friend and her sons to the Mets game, and they'd pick up Will on the way to the stadium."

"Maybe it's Sam Kaufman and his boys."

"No, I'm sure he said 'her.'" She wiped the counter with efficient swipes of the dishcloth. "Haven't I said that he's been happier these last few weeks than he's been in a long time? He must be seeing someone, Arthur."

"Well, if you're curious, why don't you ask him? 'Steve, are you dating?' It's that simple. Then you'd know, one way or the other." He shook his head at the ways of women and turned his attention to the editorials.

"I know I shouldn't worry. I tell myself he's a grown man, but I don't know—think of Elisa."

"Yes, dear, I often do." He looked up from the paper. "I hear car doors. That's probably them."

Barbara hurried into the living room and pulled aside the curtain covering the front window.

"Yes, there they are. Oh, my, she isn't even Jewish. And look at those boys."

"Isn't even Jewish?" Arthur said, coming up behind her. "How do you know?"

"I know."

"What sort of thing is that for you to say, anyway? I can't remember the last time you were at temple. What do you care if she's Jewish or not?" He peered out the window at the woman coming up the walk with Steve. "Looks respectable to me." He ignored his wife's expelled breath. "And the kids are okay--they're staying off the grass."

"It's a nice house, Steven, friendly. Did you grow up here?" Lizzie said as they followed the boys up the walk.

"I think I was about Harry's age when we moved here. How does a house look friendly?"

"I don't know," she said in surprise. "Don't some houses look friendlier than others?"

"I never gave it much thought." He opened the door and preceded her, holding the door for her and the boys, while calling out,
"Hello!"

"Here you are. I was afraid you ran into traffic." Steven's
mother hurried into the hall, her hands stretched out in welcome.
She was followed by his father, who was chuckling.

"Look at you, a regular sports team with all those caps," he said.

Mrs. Heller was a handsome woman of medium height with
short, crisp gray hair framing her face. Steven's father, newspaper
in hand and reading glasses perched just below the bridge of his
nose, had a wide smile for them. Always worried about meeting
anyone's parents, Lizzie was relieved by the warmth of the greeting.

"My fault, Mom. I got held up at the hospital. Lizzie, this is my
mother, Barbara, and my dad, Arthur. This is Lizzie Donnely, and
these are her sons, Hugh and Harry."

"Mrs. and Mr. Heller, it's good to meet you," Lizzie said, and
was glad to see that both of the boys shook hands politely. A politician's children were subjected to many introductions, and Bo had
schooled his sons well.

"Where's Will? Ah, there you are," Steve said, spying a small
figure standing in the doorway to the kitchen.

The boy, staring at Lizzie, came slowly over to the group at the
door.

Steve bent and kissed him. "Will, this is Mrs. Donnely."

Lizzie knelt to the boy's level. Small for his age and aided in
both ears with a body hearing aid, he peered at her through John
Lennon glasses. He had his father's warm brown eyes, but his face
was elfin, the features delicate.

"Will, I'm especially glad to meet you," Lizzie said, putting out her right hand.

Without taking his eyes off her face, he grasped her hand and held on to it with both of his.

"Can I call you by your real name?" he asked, his voice surprisingly deep and husky for such a small child, the articulation careful.

"Yes, you may. Your dad calls me Lizzie, but lots of people call me Liz or Elizabeth. Which do you like?"

"I think Elizabeth. It's nice and long. My real name is William."

"And do you like to be called that?"

He laughed, sounding very much like Steven. "No one does, except Gramma, when she's really mad at me."

"Which isn't very often, I hope," Liz said seriously.

"No," he said, shaking his head earnestly, "hardly ever at all. I'm pretty much a good kid."

"I thought so. You look to me like a real good kid." She stood up and put her free hand on Hugh's shoulder. "This is one of my good kids—this is Hugh," and touching Harry's shoulder, she added, "and this is the other one, this is Harry."

Steve pointed the three boys in the direction of the car and, kissing his mother, turned down her offer of ice tea. "Harry'll never forgive me if we miss that first pitch."

10

LEGS

AN EXPLOSION OF LAUGHTER, SHRIEKS, AND SHOUTING came from the back of the house. "Hold on a sec, Jen." Lizzie set the phone down and, crossing the kitchen, leaned over the sink to peer through the window but found her view blocked by the thick greenery of rose bushes.

Returning to the phone, she said, "I don't know, Jen, it's the kids, and I think Steven is out there, but I can't see them from the window. The roses need to be trimmed."

"Steven is there? What exactly is going on with this Steven thing? Do you like the guy?"

"Yes, I like him. What do you mean, 'going on'? You make it sound illegal."

Jen laughed. "I think you mean immoral. I mean, are you dating, are you serious. . .what's going on?"

"I guess what we do is 'hang out,' as the kids say. He's separated from his wife, and I live in a child's world. I think we both enjoy having adult company."

"Oh, boy. Liz, one of these days you're going to have to enter the real world. Guys don't hang out with girls just to have adult company. Unless, of course, that includes sex. And you tell me you've never even kissed? Which is hard to believe—I know, I know, you swore you weren't lying, but what? Something's wrong with him? Wait—is he gay?"

"I don't know, I guess he could be. Sexual orientation isn't one of our big topics of conversation, but I don't think so. What's so strange about two adults having a friendship? I like him. He's fun to be with, he's smart, he puts up with my kids. Now, I'd better find out what's going on out there."

"Hold on. If he's your friend, and I'm your friend, how come we've never met? He could be eighty years old, for all I know—is that it, he's old?"

"He's forty, Jen. He's average height, not skinny, not fat, he has dark hair and eyes—if he were an animal, he'd be a bear. And he has a laugh that just bursts out all joyous and free, so that it makes you happy, even if you're tired or depressed."

"Aha! Now you sound like a woman in love."

"Don't be ridiculous," Lizzie snapped. "I've told you—that isn't going to happen."

"Yeah, like it's really something you can control."

"Let's drop it, okay? I hear them again. I'm going to run."

Outside she found Hugh and his friend Michael in the driveway, working on the go-cart they'd been trying for over a year to get running. It was a perpetual project, Lizzie and Michael's mother agreed, one that kept them out of trouble.

"What's all the noise out here?" she asked.

Hugh looked up and wiped the perspiration off his forehead with his arm. "Harry was messing with the hose. He's got Steve checking out that pool thing he dug that he thinks he's going to put fish in."

"Okay, well, start thinking about dinner. Are you staying, Michael?"

"Uh-uh, because my uncle's coming to our house, and he's just home from Paris, France. But thanks for asking me, Mrs. Donnely."

"Okay, Michael. You'll stay another time."

She continued toward the back yard. Harry's voice, running up and down the scale in excited tones, and the frenzied barks of both dogs grew louder as she approached. Rounding the house, she came face to face with Steven, who was heading for the driveway.

"Hey," she said, "I didn't know you were here. . .until. . .until. . .I heard your laugh. . . ." Her voice faded. She was staring at his legs. He was barefoot with his pant legs rolled up to his knees, his legs and feet dripping wet.

He looked down. "I know. Blame your son. He's dug a fish-pond and—" He looked closely at her as she continued to stare at his legs and feet. "Lizzie? What's wrong?"

His feet were well formed and tan, as were his legs, and she knew that if she touched them, they would be cold from the hosing Harry had given them. She could see the individual hairs adhering to the skin and—she forced her eyes away, looking up at him.

"I'm sorry. Would you. . .are you eating dinner with us?"

"Thanks for the invitation, but I have a lot of calls to make. I dropped by to return your sweater. You left it in the car after the game on Saturday—Lizzie, are you all right? You look flushed." They were walking toward the front porch.

She concentrated on looking straight ahead and breathing evenly. "No. I mean, I'm fine." She touched her cheeks. "Sunburn—from the game."

On the porch he sat down on the swing, where he'd left his socks and shoes. Taking one of the socks, he wiped a wet leg and foot. He looked up at her.

She tried to work her mouth into a confident smile. "I'd better check on dinner. Thanks. Thanks for my sweater." She took it off the arm of the chair where he'd left it. "I'll see you, Steven."

Inside she put her hands to her face and bent forward as though in pain. Straightening, she hurried into the bathroom off the den and closed the door. In the mirror she checked her face and saw that her cheeks were stained a deep red. What had occurred out there? She'd seen Bo's legs a million times.

She leaned against the sink, her heart racing. Okay, she'd turned the corner of the house and had come upon Steven unexpectedly. Was that it? He'd taken her by surprise? No, this wasn't surprise—she knew what it was. She was aroused, sexually aroused—and by Steven's *legs!* God! How pitiful! She put her hands over her face, and felt the heat still rising off her skin. It was all Jen's damn fault, Jen raising the idea of sex. She leaned down and turned on the faucet, splashing water onto her burning cheeks as though its coolness, its very wetness would wash away the feelings that the sight of those bare legs had turned loose. Except, as she knew too well, the feelings weren't rising from her cheeks. And she'd been so sure she was finished with all that.

11

GOOD NIGHT

LIZZIE HADN'T HEARD FROM STEVEN since he returned her sweater. She knew he was busy with paperwork for the study he and Sam Kaufman hoped to set up at the hospital, and knew that she should be welcoming the time it gave her to deal with feelings that seemed to be surfacing exponentially. But she was edgy, and his silence was creating a void in her life. Trying to sort through what it all meant was the only way she knew to organize and gain some control over her emotional life. Only it didn't seem to be working.

The week slid by. On Friday Angelica left for the weekend, and Lizzie ordered pizza for the boys, who were joined by Hugh's friend, Michael.

"Salad?" Hugh groaned. "I thought we were going to have pizza."

"First some salad. It's Italian to go with the pizza. You can even put Italian dressing on it." She set three glass bowls brimming with greens on the table.

"Okay, but it's a damn—I mean darn—sneaky way to get fresh vegetables into us," he grumbled.

"I like salad," Harry announced from across the table.

"Shut up, dope." This from Hugh.

"Okay, stop right there," Lizzie intervened. "You're at the dinner table, you have a guest, and you will be pleasant. Am I right?"

"Yes, Mom, dear."

"Yes, sweet, adorable Mom. Now can we have our pizza?" Hugh asked. Seeing Lizzie's raised eyebrows, he added, "Please?"

"For such cooperative and polite guys, one double cheese pizza coming up."

"I see I'm just in time for dinner." Steven had appeared in the doorway.

Over the theatrical groans of the boys, he said to Lizzie, "I rang, but the bell must not be working."

She lifted her shoulders in a gesture of resignation. "One more thing to fix. What about my watchdogs?"

He walked over to the door to the den and beckoned to her. "Check them out."

Lizzie looked at Mickey and Biz curled up at opposite ends of the couch. "Terrific." She pointed to a glass on the counter. "I was about to pour myself a beer. Want one?"

He hesitated. "Okay. Then I'm going to head home. For some reason, eighty per cent of my patients decided this was the week to be sick or want their annual check-up. I'm really beat."

They took their beers into the den while the boys ate. There were more stretches of silence than conversation, and Lizzie was tempted to ask him why he had bothered to stop in. When he drank the last of his beer and rose, she said, "I'll walk out with you."

Despite the drifts and piles of fall leaves, it felt like a summer evening on Stelfox Street. Doors and windows were open to unseasonable breezes, allowing the muted sounds of voices and televisions to join the background of cricket song.

Lizzie sank down onto the porch steps. "I hope next week is quieter for you." He sat down beside her; she breathed in the antiseptic smell of doctors' offices that he wore like after-shave.

"I'm taking Will out to California next week."

She turned and looked at him. "Really? Everything's okay, I hope."

He was silent for a few moments, then said quietly, "Everything's okay."

"When do you leave?"

"Monday. I'm going to cover for Sam over the week-end."

"Where will you go in California?"

"We'll spend a few days with my sister in San Francisco, then fly down to LA."

"That'll be great for Will, to see family. Does your sister have children?"

"Three girls, all older than Will, but he needs to see them once in awhile."

"I know. I worry about my boys growing up without seeing their grandparents. How about Disney Land?"

"Oh, yeah. Will has that all mapped out."

Lizzie smiled. "Good for Will. You'll be wishing for those sick patients by the time he trots you around that park."

"You're probably right." He got up.

"Send me a postcard." She didn't know what else to say.

He turned, gazed down at her for a moment, then bent and, cupping her face in his hands, kissed her.

Lizzie's eyes widened, then closed, her mouth yielded, and she put a hand to the back of his head, drawing him closer, as a wave of desire and need engulfed her. It was a kiss that seemed to last and last, yet one that was over too soon.

"Good night, Lizzie," he said softly. He kissed her forehead, turned, and walked to his car.

"I'll miss you, Steven." The words, unbidden, hung in the night air.

12

UPSTAIRS

THE NEXT MORNING STEVE PHONED LIZZIE from the office. "We're still friends?"

"Yes. . .I'm glad you called."

"And that's because. . . ?"

"To wish you a good trip."

He sagged back in his chair. "Oh. . .that was it?"

"No. One other matter. About the kiss. . . ."

"Yes?"

"Just. . .that I loved it. You're a good kisser, Steven."

He grinned. "You, too."

The days were still unseasonably warm in New Jersey when Steve and Will returned, and the nights held no hint of the coming winter. Steve didn't see Lizzie until the end of the week, making it

two weeks they'd been apart. He seesawed between deep contentment, feeling he'd overcome a barrier he was afraid had been insur-
mountable, and an anxiety born of knowing that an occasional kiss
wasn't what he'd had in mind. He'd thought he was going to walk
away from the relationship, go to California for a week and return
to his old life of a lot of work and week-ends with Will. But now
he knew he couldn't take that walk. She was his future. There was
no way he could imagine a life without her.

It was after eight on Friday evening when he pulled into the
driveway on Stelfox. He'd spent late Thursday night and most of
Friday morning at the hospital, and the rest of the day seeing
patients in the office. He should have canceled their dinner and
gone home to bed, but his desire to see Lizzie overpowered his
need for sleep.

The front door was open, the screen unlatched. He rang and
went in, patting wagging dogs as he made his way to the kitchen.
The house was still, no music or television blaring, no little boy
sounds, and no one in the kitchen or den. "Lizzie?" he shouted.

"In here."

He found her in the dining room, where the chandelier was
casting soft light over a partially set table. She was kneeling on the
floor, surrounded by a glimmering circle of glass shards that he
realized had been the salad bowl and by a mound of brightly colored vegetables—the salad itself.

"I tripped," she said before he could ask.

"Where's the vacuum? Don't try to pick it up, you're going to
cut yourself."

"I want to get the big pieces. I'm being careful, I won't—oh!"
She pulled her hand back.

"Okay. Let me see it." He took her arm and helped her up. Blood welled from under the nail on her right index finger.

"It's okay," she said and reached for a napkin on the table, winding it around the bleeding finger. "Look at this mess! And I really wanted to have an elegant welcome home dinner for you."

He took her hand and removed the napkin. "Hold still. Let me see if there's glass under your nail." He blotted the blood and examined her finger. "No, it looks clean. Let's wash it. . ." She had stepped closer, and he saw her eyes lose their focus as she leaned in to kiss him.

He wrapped her in his arms, held her tight, buried his face in her neck and kissed her eyes, her cheeks, her lips, her skin, warmer and softer than he had dreamed. He breathed her in with deep, hungry breaths. She moved further into his embrace, repeating his name, her breath coming in gasps. He ran his hands down her, pulling her against him, felt her fingers making a path through his hair.

"Come upstairs with me," he whispered. "It's time."

Lizzie knew the exact moment when she gave him her heart. It wasn't during the bliss and relief of their love making, but afterwards, when his eyelids drifted shut, and his lips parted slightly, and he slept. She outlined his features with her fingertips, ran her lips from his brow to his chin.

"This wasn't supposed to happen, Steven," she said softly. "Now what will I do?"

13

PRAY

The following Monday, as soon as her ten boys were aboard their buses, Lizzie left school and drove across town to Christ Church, where she found Todd Parker, the church secretary, hunched over his keyboard, eyes glued to the monitor.

"Is she free, Todd?"

He swung around to face her, pushing a thin fall of dark hair off his forehead. "Liz! I didn't hear you come in. Yes, she is. Shall I let her know you're here?"

"No, please don't bother. I'll just go on in."

The rector's study was bright, cheerful, and, it seemed to Lizzie, always skirting the edge of being cluttered. Annie West was sitting at her desk in front of a row of high, narrow, many-paned windows. Two upholstered chairs and a love seat were arranged around a cof-

fee table, while the walls were lined with floor-to-ceiling bookcas-
es, filled to the point of overflowing.

"What a welcome surprise," Annie exclaimed, pushing her
glasses up into her graying hair. "A day of teaching and you still
manage to look radiant. Amazing. Can you stay? Because I'd love
a break from this diocesan report." She gestured to the sprawl of
papers that occupied most of the desktop.

Lizzie nodded. "I was hoping you could spare me a few minutes. And your ear, because I think I have a moral problem."

"Oh, dear, on such a beautiful autumn day. Let's go into the
kitchen and get a cup of tea. Then we'll talk."

Sitting cross legged on the couch in the rector's study, holding one
of the church's thick earthenware cups with both hands, Lizzie
studied Annie and wondered if her own face would grow to look so
wise.

"Shall we put your problem on the table and have a go at it?"

Lizzie nodded. "Steven and I had sex."

"Ah. And you wanted your priest to know this because. . . ?"

Lizzie shook her head, embarassed. "Sorry. That did sound idi-
otic." She turned the cup round and round between her hands and
watched the steam swirl. "It worries me. A married man. A widow
with two children. I mean, for all I know it could get me ex-com-
municated. . .or whatever we do in our church with people who dis-
regard its teachings."

"Well, we don't often speak in terms of ex-communication, but
it's true that premarital sex isn't something we go around beating
the drum for. Still, it can be a way for committed partners to
become comfortable with the idea of marriage—"

"Wait!" Lizzie interrupted. "Premarital? No, no, no," she said, waving a hand. "You see, that's part of the problem. Steven is already married. What?" she said, as Annie's eyebrows rose. "Okay, separated, but, trust me, we're not thinking of marriage. And the thing is, Annie, the thing is. . . ." She stopped and looked away.

"The thing is?" Annie prompted.

"The thing is. . .I want it to continue." She swung her gaze to meet Annie's. "The sex."

"I can understand that. You're a healthy young woman. And Steve is a desirable man. Have you asked him how he feels about marriage?"

Lizzie, caught in the midst of sipping tea, sat up straight, coughing. Mopping up, she shook her head. "No, you don't understand. I couldn't. He'd think I was suggesting. . .well, I'm not considering marriage, so I can't discuss it."

Annie thought a moment. "Do you love him, Liz?"

Lizzie narrowed her eyes and sat very still. "I don't know," she finally admitted. "The problem is, I don't know about love. I know I love my children, but. . . ."

"Yes?"

She shook her head. "I'm very fond of Steven, and, now. . .well, what is it I feel? Is it just a physical thing, or loneliness, or is it love?" She looked at the motes of dust dancing in the sun that slanted through the windows behind Annie and was aware of the stillness that lay over the study like a comforting blanket. "I loved Bo," she said softly, "and what happened to it? Did it die? You see, I just don't know."

"That complicates things, doesn't it?"

Lizzie rolled her eyes. "For sure. I need a little help here. I mean, if we continue this relationship, am I going to wake up one morning and despise myself. . .or despise him?"

Annie sat back in her chair, the touch of a wry smile softening her face. "Thanks for your faith in my abilities, but I really don't predict the future. And I'm not going to hand out a by-the-book number of prayers for you to utter and send you off with a 'Go and sin no more' message." She set her cup aside and leaned forward. "I do, however, recommend that you pray about it."

Lizzie groaned. "Ah, Annie, we've talked about prayer before. Specifically, my lack of success with it, as far as receiving any kind of direction."

"Umm, so we have. And I always remind you that it's not going to be a resounding bass voice, giving you specifics, that you'll hear. Meditate. Ponder. Contemplate. Don't even think of it as prayer. Just be open."

Lizzie sighed. "Okay. Okay, I'll do it."

"Good. I have people coming at four, so I have to kick you out." She stood and walked with Lizzie to the door. "Keep me posted."

14

STARBUCKS

IT WAS THE LAST MONDAY IN OCTOBER. Daylight savings
time had ended, but summer seemed loath to die and persisted,
stubborn for such a benevolent season. The warm, September-like
temperatures had continued, the sky a cloudless, vivid blue. But
Halloween was just days away, and Steve still hadn't bought the
mask Will had asked for, the one he'd seen in Barrow's Variety
Store on Cedar Avenue a few weeks earlier, when they stopped for
ice cream on their way back to Queens. It had been a Sunday, and
Barrow's was closed.

"You're sure you know which one I want? The fuzzy monster,
not the one with green lumps all over it?"

"I know, Will, that one on the end, right?" Steve had said,
pointing with his cone.

"That's it, Daddy. You'll get it? You won't forget?"

"Absolutely not. I won't forget."

It was down to the wire. He left the office as soon as he'd seen the last of his morning patients, Eliot Hermann, who had droned on and on about the price of his prescriptions, which with increasing regularity he forgot to take, and walked the mile and a half to Barrow's. Walking felt good, stretching his legs and filling his lungs to capacity—something hopping in and out of the car, which he did on a daily basis, never accomplished. When he came out of Barrow's, the fuzzy monster mask purchased and bagged, he hesitated, thinking that he might as well cross over to the deli and pick up a sandwich and a latte at Starbucks, a few doors down from the deli. Looking to his left before crossing mid-block, he froze. That's what it felt like, ice water pouring over his head, pooling in his chest cavity.

Lizzie was sitting at one of the outdoor tables at Starbucks, the sun dancing off her hair in quick, golden darts. And at the table with her, a tall, lean George Clooney double, who must have said something particularly clever, for Lizzie was laughing and inclining her head toward his, her hand resting on his forearm.

Steve stepped back from the curb, unable to take his eyes off them. Why wasn't she in school? Who. . .but he stopped himself, and, forcing his breathing to return to normal, turned right and headed back to the office.

On the following Friday evening Steve sat in his favorite wing chair in Lizzie's living room. He had tried all week to distract himself from thinking about the Starbucks scene, which was how he thought of it, but nothing worked. His brain was stuck on 'replay,' and he'd had to endure seeing her hair in the sunlight, her laughing face, her hand on the guy's arm, had to watch it over and over again.

"Hey, Steve." Harry came in and flopped down on the couch.

Steve was glad to have his thoughts interrupted.

"Hey, Harry. How was Halloween?"

"Great. I got so much candy, you should see. Want some? 'Cause I got lots."

"No, I think I'll pass, but thanks for the offer. Bet your mom isn't thrilled about you eating all that candy."

Shooting him a conspiratorial smile and casting a quick glance at the doorway, the child lowered his voice and said, "She's not, but she loves the KitKat bars, so I bribe her."

Steve bit his lip. "KitKat bars, huh? I see."

Harry focused on his left sneaker, which had a small rip along the sole. "Do you like my mom, Steve?"

"Yes. Yes, I do."

"She's not married, you know." He tugged at the piece of rubber.

"I know that, Harry. I'm real sorry about your dad."

"He was a senator. I forget now what he did, being a senator and all."

"Yeah, it's a complicated sort of job, but an important one."

"Here I am. Sorry I'm running so late." Lizzie hurried into the room. "Harry! I've been looking for you. Angelica needs some help in the basement, sweetie. Give her a hand, will you?"

Harry pushed himself off the couch. "Okay, but remember? No more 'sweeties.'"

"Oh, right. I forgot. Good night, Harry. Is that better?"

"Uh-huh, better. Night, Mom." He kissed her and accepted

her hug, then went over to the chair, put his arms around Steve's neck and kissed his cheek. "Night, Steve."

When he had disappeared, Steve said, "No 'sweeties,' but hugs and kisses are still allowed?"

Lizzie smiled and handed him her coat. "I think the 'no sweeties' is the first step. Sadly, the hugs and kisses will probably follow."

As he settled the coat on her shoulders, he had an overpowering desire to kiss the nape of her neck. He resisted and wondered if it was because of the lean, handsome stranger—and the suspicions that had been burning a hole in his gut all week.

They were both unusually quiet on the drive into the city. Lizzie looked tired, Steve thought, even preoccupied. God, what if she was going to tell him she'd made a mistake allowing their relationship to deepen, that she wanted out of it, wanted to see someone else? His stomach hurt, joining his already aching head. And he had wanted this to be a special evening. They were going to Pete's, a small jazz club in the Village.

He put the car in a nearby lot, and they scurried through a cold rain, not heavy but driven by a strong wind. The mellow Indian summer days had ended the day before with a wave of cold air from Canada. Inside the entrance he helped her out of her coat.

"Good holy Jesus! Look what the rain drove in!" A wiry black man threw his arms around Steve.

"Hey, Pete!" Steve cried, thumping the man's back.

He had a grizzled head and eyes set deep amid a myriad of laugh lines. "Where in all God's creation have you been? I thought sure we'd seen the last of your sorry ass." He turned to Lizzie. "You with this sad excuse of a man?" At her nod he moved his head back and forth slowly to a funereal beat. "Little lady, you and me better have a talk before you leave here tonight, hear? 'Cause I got some serious revelations to share with you before you get in too deep with this guy." He hugged Steve again, his face wreathed in affection.

"Pete, how the hell are you? You look good," Steve said, holding him by the shoulders at arms' length and studying him. "You look real good."

"Damn right. Got those diabetes on the ropes. Where're you doctoring? Or did they get smart and pull your license?"

"Port Smith, over in Jersey. I'm sure I sent you an announcement when Sam and I opened our office."

Pete gestured dismissively. "Probably got tossed with the junk mail. Port Smith, huh? Too far for me to travel. You fellows doing okay? Making big bucks?"

"We're getting by." Steve put an arm around Lizzie. "This is a friend of mine, Elizabeth Donnely. She's an opera buff, doesn't know much about jazz, so I thought it was time she was introduced to some of the good stuff."

"Come to the right place." Pete held Lizzie's hand after shaking it. "Doing something right for a change. I got a good table for you."

They followed him inside, where the lights were all but extinguished and a single spot shone on a quartet playing "Dark Eyes" in the front of the room. The room itself was small, intimate, and the sour, pleasant smell of beer hung in the air. He showed them to a table against the wall and took their drink orders before leaving them.

Lizzie leaned over the table, her eyebrows raised. "What's this? You have another life, you and Sam? I knew you liked jazz, but you must have spent a lot of time here to be treated like a prodigal son."

He nodded, surveying the room, which wasn't crowded but was beginning to fill with young couples. It was still early. "Sam and I spent some time here, starting back in med school. Jazz—it's how I met Sam, you know. I admired his record collection—all jazz."

A gangly young man appeared with their drinks balanced precariously on a small, round tray aslosh with the top third of Steve's drink.

"She'll have the beer," Steve said. "I'll take the Scotch and soda."

The boy placed a cocktail napkin imprinted with the club's name in front of each of them, put a bottle of Coors and a glass in front of Lizzie, and glanced ruefully at the Scotch.

"It's okay," Steve assured him and watched him set the dripping glass in the exact center of the napkin.

"So you've known Pete a long time," Lizzie said after he'd left.

"Yeah, we go back. We found out he was having some physical problems, and Sam and I knew it all, of course, being first year med students." He grinned at his irony. "His doctor was a quack, had him taking tonics and all sorts of stuff, missing the diagnosis completely."

"What was the right one?"

"Classic symptoms of diabetes. We convinced him to go to a doctor at University Hospital. After he started feeling better, he decided we were God's gift to the medical profession."

She gazed at him, a smile hovering in her eyes. "I think so, too," she said.

"Really." He didn't intend for it to sound as nasty as it did.

Head to one side, she asked, "What's that mean?"

"Sorry. I've had a bad week."

"I wondered why you hadn't called."

He picked up his glass, ran his fingers around the bottom, then set it down. ". . .Probably a small thing, but it's been driving me crazy since Monday."

"What happened Monday?" She waited. "You can't tell me?"

He considered. "I think I'd better. Otherwise it's going to keep eating at me. And disturb things between us."

"Between *us*? She frowned. "But I didn't see you on Monday."

"No. *I* saw *you*, which is the problem. At Starbucks around noon."

She frowned. "You saw me, but I didn't see you? I don't understand." Her face suddenly cleared. "Ah. I see." She looked across the table at him, her eyes narrowed.

Steve made a small, waving gesture with his right hand. "Who is he?"

"Chris. Chris Barrett."

He held her gaze, suddenly aware of how his heels were digging into the carpet beneath his chair, as though to keep him from falling over.

"Chris and I have known each other since we were children. He's married to my college roommate," she said without expression.

A hot wave of blood swept up through his chest into his face.

She continued in the same neutral tone, "His daughter Liza is my godchild. He and Anne moved to Chicago a few years ago. I haven't seen them since Katie. . .since her funeral."

"Please, I understand—"

But she was relentless. "Chris was in New York on business. I managed to get a double lunch hour, and he came over to Port Smith so we could get together, if only for an hour."

Steve nodded. "I've really screwed up." He addressed his drink. "Haven't I?"

She leaned toward him and asked softly, "Did you really think I'd see another man with us having the kind of relationship we have?"

A woman had joined the quartet and was singing "Misty". Steve considered his options. He could stick a knife in his heart and bleed to death right there in front of her; he could excuse himself, pay the check at the door and walk out of her life; or he could stay and argue that he had been justified in being suspicious, that she should have called him, told him about this childhood friend. The knife thing was out because there wasn't one in sight.

"Steven?"

"I don't know, Lizzie—I'm contemplating suicide. What can I say? An apology seems pretty lame at this point, but if it would help," he said, his voice thickening, "you have my deepest apology."

"Okay."

He looked down at his fingers, which were drumming on the edge of the table, then across at her closed face. "Can you not be angry?"

"You think I'm angry?"

"You have every right. To be angry."

She shook her head.

They listened to the music, which she seemed to be enjoying, and slowly his stomach began to feel better and his headache receded.

After a time, Pete pulled up a chair and joined them. "Not

going to play tonight, huh?" he asked Steve.

Steve met Lizzie's questioning look. "Nope. I'm afraid I'm too rusty for this crowd, Pete."

"He plays. . .what?" Lizzie asked.

Pete shot Steve an admonishing glance before turning to Lizzie. "He didn't tell you he plays one fine alto sax? Oh, yeah, him, and Sam on drums, they did good up there." He nodded toward the stage. "Sweet music. Yes, sir, real sweet."

Steve shook his head but couldn't hide a grin. "Don't listen to him—he exaggerates. What he did was humor two amateurs by letting them perform once in awhile with the pros."

"Go ahead, lie about it—if I was you, I'd brag." Standing, he said to Lizzie, "Both of them, they're good, believe me. I don't lie about music—most other things, yeah." He patted Steve on the shoulder and winked at her. "Better get back to work. Got a living to make."

When the waiter came over to refresh their drinks, Steve shook his head, thanked him, and asked for the check.

Walking to the car, Lizzie threaded her arm around his waist and said, "You're allowed to screw up now and then."

He sighed, not sure if this made him feel better or worse. He put his arm around her shoulders, pulling her close. "I know a place that sells KitKat bars in quantity, and real cheap. What do you say?"

15

SHAVING

STEVE WAS AWARE OF HARRY, leaning cheek on hand, elbow on kitchen table and solemnly regarding him as he cut up vegetables for a salad. Harry was a funny little guy, Steve thought, so serious in his curiosity about everything, the possessor of a very vulnerable heart.

"Do you shave, Steve?" he asked, breaking his silence.

"Um-hmm, yes, I do."

"Do you shave in the morning?"

"Usually, Harry."

"Every morning?"

"Well, almost every morning."

"Does it hurt?"

"Nope, not if you do it right."

"Did you ever bleed?"

"Oh, yeah, that happens."

"Not bad, though, right?"

"Right."

"Bo shaved."

"Yes, I'm sure he did."

"Does your boy watch you shave, Steve?"

"Sometimes, Harry, sometimes he watches me shave."

"Do you yell at him?"

"Yell at him?"

"Yeah, you know, if he drives you crazy."

"Oh." Steve looked over his shoulder into Harry's unwavering gaze. "No, I don't yell at him, Harry."

"You could shave here, Steve. If you wanted to."

"Shave here?" Lizzie, coming in from the den, gave Harry a questioning look.

"Harry and I were having a talk—guy stuff. Weren't we?"

"Uh-huh."

"Well, I want you to clear some floor space in your bedroom, Harry. I was up there earlier, and I don't know how you get from the door to the bed with all those Legos spread around."

"Then can I watch TV?"

"For a half hour."

"Okay! I'm out of here!"

She peered into the salad bowl. "That looks good."

"Thanks." He put the bowl on the table. "Harry misses his dad." When she didn't respond, he glanced at her and met the same unwavering gaze that Harry had given him. And he knew that further discussion on the subject wasn't going to happen.

16

DYING ELEPHANTS

"THIS IS NICE." Lizzie had settled her head against Steve's shoulder, into the hollow between his chest and arm, thinking no deeper thought than that her head seemed to have been formed exactly right for that particular part of his anatomy. He wrapped his arms around her, and she sighed. They lay together on the couch in the den, a CD playing softly.

"Why don't we do this more often?" she murmured, drugged with contentment.

He rubbed his cheek along the side of her head, taking in the smell of chalk that clung to her hair. "I think having every kid in the neighborhood running in and out of here any time of the day or night may have something to do with it."

"Think so?"

"Um-hmm."

"Well, we have another hour before the movie lets out in Port Smith and Angelica herds two of those kids home."

"Wonderful invention, the motion picture."

She smiled. "This music is beautiful, one of my favorites. *La Bohème*. Do you like opera?"

He recalled his conversation with Hugh and Harry. "Dying elephants," he murmured and was surprised to feel her whole body stiffen.

"What did you say?"

"Not important—something Harry said."

She sat up and pushed away from him. "No, tell me." Her face was stricken.

"Lizzie, really, it's nothing." He reached for her, but she drew back. "What is it?"

She didn't say anything, and he saw that her lips were trembling.

"Lizzie," he said softly and pulled her against his chest. "What did I say? The boys told me that Bo thought opera sounded like dying elephants, and it popped into my head when you asked. That's all."

She drew a long, shuddering breath. In the background Mimi was singing her aria of longing.

"Maybe you want to tell me what the big mystery is," Steve said. "Now that I think about it, my conversation with Hugh and Harry was a little strange."

"It's not some big mystery, just. . .a family quarrel."

"About opera?"

"Yes. . .no. It. . .it was more than a quarrel. More. . .like a family secret."

"Ah. I see. Do you want to talk about it—this family secret?"

She felt his chest move slowly with each breath he drew, like waves washing in and out. She didn't want to lose the comfort and peace of these rare moments together but realized she already had. The memory of that long-past afternoon was in her head so vividly that Wagner's rich, voluminous notes shoved Puccini's aside.

"I don't know. I never have. . .but. . .maybe I need to tell you."

He waited. Just when he thought she wasn't going to explain, she began. "It was a couple months before the plane crash—before Bo died. Those last months were hard on him. He was concentrating all his energy on campaigning. There were always people around him—aides, volunteers, reporters. He was never alone, it seemed, never had any quiet time. But he wanted that House seat so badly, and it looked like he had a strong chance of getting it. The polls put him slightly ahead. Maybe that made for more pressure, I don't know." She moved her hands along Steve's forearms.

"Anyway, there was a big parade in Newark on Memorial Day. Bo and I were scheduled to be there, and he was going to speak at the services following the parade.

"But Katie got one of her earaches a couple days before, and I had been up with her for three nights. I begged off." She paused for a long moment, cleared her throat, then continued, "He wasn't happy about it. Looking back, I know I should have gone with him."

"You stayed home."

"I did. After he left for Newark, Katie finally settled down. And the boys were working on a puzzle in the den. It was peaceful. You see, for months the house had been noisy and chaotic—

phones ringing constantly, his staff in and out, fax machines going—it was madness. It was hard on all of us.

"But that afternoon it was quiet. I listened to an opera on the radio while I made potato salad for dinner. Bo got home earlier than I had expected. I didn't hear him come in, or I would have switched stations. They were playing Wagner's *Flying Dutchman*. You have to understand—Bo hated operatic music. As you know, he told the boys it sounded like dying elephants. And for some rea- son he couldn't stand my loving it. Anyhow, he stormed into the kitchen and said something like, did I want to hear that music? 'I can make sure you hear it!' he said, and he turned it to full volume." She was still.

"What happened?"

Her head dug into his shoulder. "It was as if. . .as if a bomb had exploded. I tried to turn it off. Wagner's thunderous enough as it is. The sound was deafening. Hugh and Harry came racing in, screaming, and I could hear Katie shrieking, but Bo. . .he wouldn't let me near the radio."

Her voice was stretched to the breaking point. "Bo. . .the poor kids. . . ."

She waited until her breathing slowed. "He. . .he grabbed the bowl of potato salad and flung it to the floor. Then the radio. . .he threw it across the room. It hit the wall—burst into a million pieces. Parts flew everywhere. Harry and I—I guess we were stunned, but Hugh. . .oh, Hugh went crazy. He flew at Bo. . .start- ed punching him, kicking, screaming—I tried to grab him." Her fingers dug into Steve's arms. "Bo pushed me aside, knocked Harry across the floor. The dogs were barking, racing back and forth." She shuddered. "Then Bo took Hugh by the hair and . . .and he lifted him. . .lifted him right off the floor. He'd never even spanked him before, so. . . ."

"He spanked him?"

She shook her head.

"Lizzie?"

"He beat him," she whispered.

"He beat him. Jesus."

"I finally managed to stop him. . .but by then. . .we had to take Hugh to the emergency room."

Steve rocked her in his arms.

"And Bo lied. . .the media. . .child abuse. . . ." She wiped her eyes with her fingers. "It would have been the end of his political career. He told the doctor the boys had been fighting. . .with one another. Imagine the doctor believing little Harry—he was only three— could do such damage. It was awful."

They lay there, listening to Rudolfo's haunting refrain as he knelt beside the dying Mimi.

17

DAD

"Harry, guess who came to my office today?" It was a Friday evening in early December, and Steve was stretched out on the floor in the Donnelys' den, assisting Harry in a delicate Lego operation. Would Harry succeed in building a miniature Empire State Building or would gravity rule the day? That was the question facing the two engineers.

"Put your other hand on this side, Steve. I think we got it, if I can just. . . ." Harry's voice trailed off as he put every bit of his Lego know-how into righting the swaying structure.

Steve loved to watch Harry work. The boy invested all of himself in whatever project he was tackling, and his face was a mirror of his singular purpose.

"Don't you want to know who my patient was?"

"I do, Steve. Who?" Harry spoke with his lower lip caught between his teeth, making his voice sound gritty.

"It was Santa Claus." Steve kept his face turned to the building, but his eyes cut to his left to catch Harry's reaction.

"Santa Claus?" Harry's voice rose. "He was in your office, Steve?"

"Careful now, or we'll lose this baby. Yep. This afternoon."

Lizzie came in wearing a bright-blue down vest and mittens, carrying an armful of logs. "Cold in here, don't you think?" she said, checking the thermostat on the wall inside the door.

"Mom! Guess who was in Steve's office—don't tell, Steve. Guess, Mom! Come on, guess!"

Lizzie put the logs down on the hearth and shrugged out of the vest. "Who was in Steve's office? Let me see, was it a man or a woman?"

"No, Mom!" Harry groaned. "Not 'Twenty Questions!'" He scrambled to his feet, abandoning the tower. "Just guess! No, I'll tell you. Steve says Santa Claus was there. In his office. This afternoon." He plunked down on the couch.

Lizzie, kneeling in front of the fireplace, looked sharply at Steve, who raised his eyebrows and nodded.

"Was it really him? Was it, Steve? Hugh says there are too many Santas to be real. He says, 'Use your head, Fred!'"

"Hugh has a point. You have to use your head, but you also have to trust." Steve knelt beside Lizzie, aware that she was giving him a 'you better know what you're doing' look. "I'll do this," he told her, taking a log from her hands.

"You see, Harry, this guy—and, boy, he was a chubby fellow—was sitting in the examining room. He had on the red suit and the beard and all the Santa Claus stuff. He even had red cheeks. Of course, he had a temperature of a hundred and two. But anyhow, here's the thing. He said that, sure enough, he was a Santa Claus, but not the real Santa Claus, who, he said, stayed in the North Pole until Christmas Eve."

Harry gave this some thought, swinging his legs and studying the buckle of his belt. "So what does this guy do?"

Steve studied the arrangement of logs and kindling he'd built, then held a flame to the kindling. "The real Santa sends lots of Santas all over the world to do good deeds, because he has to stay at the North Pole and make sure all the toys get made. The Santa in my office—his good deed is to stand beside a big black pot on the street in front of the Port Smith Post Office." Satisfied that the fire was going, he got to his feet and put the screen in front of it before joining Harry on the couch. "He rings a bell and says lots of 'Ho, ho, hoes' and 'Merry Christmases' and hopes people will put money in the pot. Because that money is needed to help a lot of little kids have a happy Christmas."

"Yeah?"

"Uh-huh. Really."

"What about his temperchur? Did you give him some medicine?"

"I gave him prescriptions for antibiotics and cough syrup and told him to stay indoors and rest for a week until he was better."

"Do you have trust in the real Santa?"

"Yep, because I always get presents for Christmas."

"I do, too!" Harry sat up straight. "I think I'll use my head, and I'll trust. Like you. Does Will get presents?"

"Sure does. Now, let's get the Empire State Building finished, because your mom is looking at the clock, and you know what that means."

"Uh-huh." He slid to the floor and approached the swaying structure on his knees. "Bedtime."

After Harry went up to bed and Lizzie followed to tuck him in for the night, Steve leaned back, settled his feet on the coffee table, and allowed himself to consider the enormity of his contentment. It was something he usually made a practice of not doing, because, while he wasn't a superstitious person, he viewed his relationship with Lizzie as so vital to his well-being that he feared putting it under a microscope might jeopardize it.

Sleet tapped delicately at the windows, and branches of the dogwood scraped the side of the house. Inside the lamplight glowed softly, lending a patina to the old wood paneling on the walls. From below came the pleasant grumble of the furnace.

"You look ready to fall asleep," Lizzie said, taking Harry's place on the couch.

"Nope, just relaxed." He pulled her close and, lifting her hair, kissed her neck. "Where did you say Hugh was?"

"Michael's. Home any minute."

"Umm. Not that I don't love Hugh, but, damn, Lizzie, we have a logistics problem here."

"You don't like being friends?"

He laughed. "Okay, we'll be friends."

"I think you shored up Harry's belief in Santa Claus. This is probably his last year for that, especially with Hugh teaching him about the real world."

"Yeah. It doesn't last long, but it's sure magical while it does. What would you like Santa to bring you for Christmas?" he asked.

"Did you celebrate Christmas when you were little?"

He thought about this. "Well, we had a tree and got presents, but it was a little tricky, being Jewish. My dad has this thing for Christmas trees. He used us as an excuse to have one every year, and now he has Will. 'A kid has to have a tree, Barbara,'" he said in Arthur Heller's voice. "How about you? Do you go to Philadelphia?"

"For Christmas? No, we've always stayed here." She stretched her legs, getting her feet closer to the warmth coming from the fireplace. "Mother and Dad used to spend it with us."

"They don't come anymore?"

She shook her head. "My dad hasn't spoken to me since Bo died. He won't come here, and Mother won't come without him."

Steve took a moment to consider this new piece of Lizzie's history. "Really. But you were at your mother and dad's for Thanksgiving. He didn't speak to you?"

"No. Well, he speaks. You know—'Pass the gravy,' that sort of 'speak,' but otherwise I get the cold shoulder." She pulled away from him so that she could see his face. "He won't look at me. I think that's the thing that bothers me most." She drew an index finger along the frown lines between his eyes. "I'm sorry. I'm so used to my dad's behavior that I forget it shocks people."

"Not shock—well, maybe surprise. Do you want to tell me *why* he hasn't spoken to you since Bo died?"

"I would if I could, but I can't." She paused. "I'm not being silly. The truth is, I don't know. Maybe he thinks I should have been in that plane with Bo—like a good wife. Everything having to do with my dad has its twists and turns. There are no simple answers. He loved Bo like the son he never had, and Bo's death was devastating for him."

"So *he* needed comforting, not you."

She nodded. "Especially not me. My dad and I. . .we have a history."

"You've never gotten along?"

"No, it's not that. He was my first—maybe my best teacher. But I think he lost interest in me when he realized I wasn't going to study law. Did you know he's a lawyer?"

"No, I didn't know that. In Philadelphia?"

"William Hayford Ward of Ward, Scott, Ward, Attorneys at Law. A venerable old firm," she said with uncharacteristic bitterness. "His family is filled with lawyers and judges—his father, his brother, his uncles, his cousins. You'd think he had enough. Dad feels I failed him. Not only failed him, failed him on purpose."

"Ah. And what do you think?"

"I think I wasn't the child he hoped for, and he wasn't the father I needed."

"I see. That's very wise of you, Lizzie."

"It took me a lot of years."

"That's okay. Some people never figure out family connections. Your dad approved of Bo?"

"Oh, yes, big time. They were like father and son. Bo's parents died when he was little. He was raised by his grandmother. And, of course he was a lawyer, which put him on the path to perfection as far as Dad was concerned."

"What about your sister? Pam. She didn't go to law school. He didn't give her grief?"

"Not as much as he gave me. I guess because I was the first-born, I got the brunt of it. Also, Pam is good at being agreeable.

She agrees him to death, then does what she wants."

"And you can't do that."

It wasn't a question, but Lizzie, answered. "No. . .no, I never could."

18

CHRISTMAS

CHRISTMAS HAD ALWAYS BEGUN FOR LIZZIE, not on the day, but at eleven o'clock on Christmas Eve. As a child she had sat with her parents and sister in St. Martin-in-the-Fields on Willow Grove Avenue in Philadelphia and welcomed the Christ child with carols. At Christ Church in Port Smith the Christmas Eve liturgy began with a child standing beside the creche in the back of the church, singing a cappella the first verse of 'Once in Royal David's City.' Thick white candles cast solemn shadows over the pews, pine trees scented the air, and scarlet poinsettias stood in startling contrast against gleaming white altar hangings. Outside the night lay dark and cold as that sweet voice filled the old Gothic Revival church, and Lizzie would know that Christmas had arrived.

Climbing out of bed the next morning was another matter.

Hugh had reached an age where he would have slept on. Harry, on the other hand, generated such excitement that sleep became impossible.

"I'm dressed, Mom. I'm all ready. Can I go down? Can I wake Angelica? Did Santa come? Can I get my cereal? Please, please!"

Lizzie had difficulty focusing on him, since he appeared to be in perpetual motion.

"Harry, lie down here for a minute," she pleaded, her voice groggy with sleep. "Let me wake up. Then I'll answer your questions, one at. . .a. . .time. . . ." Her eyes drifted shut.

"Oh, no, I knew it! You're going back to sleep! Wake up, Mom, it's Christmas, and I want to see the presents!"

After the presents were opened and breakfast eaten, she took the boys to church for the quiet Christmas morning service. Angelica had insisted on cleaning up the mess they'd left in their wake, because, she'd explained, she wouldn't be able to help with dinner. Her friend Julio was taking her to his family's celebration in the Bronx.

The Hellers arrived at two. She was ready, since Steven had warned her that his father had an internal clock that kept perfect time. Having prepared the greater part of the dinner beforehand, she had raised the subject of appropriate language with Hugh and reminded Harry that he was a host and would need to show Will every consideration. Hugh had built towers of logs and kindling in both fireplaces, and now the flames were dancing and spitting. The tree had been decorated by the boys with ornaments accumulated over fifteen years, including several strange-looking ones that the children had made in years past. The tree was just the way Lizzie liked it, but she was afraid it would disappoint Arthur

Heller, presenting as it did such a homey appearance. As it turned out, that was the way he liked it, too.

"Great tree! I like this tree!" were his first words inside the house.

Will, his eyes wide and reflecting the tree lights, his arms windmilling in excitement, hopped around it. "It's big, and look at this!" he cried. "A real sea shell—with sparkles on it!" The shell, a preschool effort of Hugh's, so heavy that it had to be looped over several branches, was admired by everyone.

The Hellers were the kind of guests all hosts hope for: at ease themselves, they helped everyone relax and have a good time. After presents were exchanged, they went into the den with the children to play Hugh's new game of Concentration. Lizzie and Steve lingered in front of the fire.

"Mom!" Harry barreled in, putting on brakes when he saw them. "Hey," he said, his eyes narrowing with suspicion. "You two were kissing."

"Yes, we were, Harry," Steve said, standing and putting out a hand to Lizzie. "It's an old custom. You have to kiss the hostess, or you don't get Christmas dinner. So I guess I get dinner. How about you? Have you kissed your mother today?"

Harry looked from Steve to Lizzie. "I can't remember. Did I, Mom, did I kiss you?"

"You'd better kiss me again, Harry, just to be on the safe side." She held him tight for a moment. "Merry Christmas, sweetheart," she murmured into the warm fold between his neck and shoulder.

Barbara and Lizzie chased everyone down to the ping pong table in the basement between the main course and dessert, while they cleared the table and brought order to the kitchen. Lizzie felt comfortable working with Barbara, admiring the older woman's quick and efficient movements in a strange kitchen.

"Dad, we're winning!" Will's delighted cry came drifting up the basement steps.

Lizzie exchanged smiles with Barbara. "They're a great father-son team," she said.

Barbara nodded. "They're very close. Did you know that Steven left his practice to care for Will after he was born? And he wasn't an easy baby. He had so many problems."

Lizzie turned from the sink where she was rinsing plates. "No, he never told me that."

"Yes, he took a year off and would have liked another, but Arthur and I urged him to leave Will with us."

"Well, together you have a really fine boy."

"I think so." Barbara began cutting wedges from the pies she had brought. "Steven will begin the new year a far happier person than he's been in a long time." She straightened and looked at Lizzie. "I believe we have you to thank for that."

Lizzie poured water into the coffee maker. She pushed the lid down on the carafe and set it on the heating element. "You don't disapprove of our relationship? I've wondered how it must seem to you—Steven being only separated. . .actually still married. I wasn't sure how a mother would feel about that."

Barbara wiped her hands on her apron. "No, my dear, I don't disapprove. You have sons. You can perhaps understand how it makes me feel to see Steven enjoying life again."

Lizzie leaned back against the counter and studied the pattern of the floor tiles, while she considered a question she needed to ask.

"I guess I don't know much about his life before we met. He'd been unhappy?"

"With Elisa? Terribly, but then. . . ." The older woman stopped and looked closely at Lizzie. "He hasn't told you about Elisa?"

"No. We—neither of us—have talked much about our marriages. I suppose because they seem to have nothing to do with. . .us, with how we get on."

"I see." Barbara began arranging plates of pie on a tray. "No, that's not true. I don't understand—but you're both smart and sensible. You must know what you're doing."

Lizzie managed a faint smile. "I'm not sure about that. . .the knowing what we're doing part."

19

TEA

ONE SUNDAY AFTERNOON IN EARLY JANUARY, Lizzie, on her way from the kitchen, heard the bell and, seeing Jen through the glass in the door, waved to her to come in. Outside the sky was glaring down on week-old snow that refused to melt, preferring instead to incorporate grime and soot into its graying mounds and slowly turn to ice. Its top layer had an oily sheen that reflected light and looked unhealthy. Winter in the suburbs had set in.

"Sorry I'm late. Hope Ian wasn't a nuisance." Jen, fighting the wind, pushed the door closed behind her. "What's that fabulous smell?" She leaned back against the door, inhaling deeply.

"Angelica's baking Hugh's birthday cake." Lizzie unwound Jen's bulky muffler from around her neck. "I can't offer you any of the cake, but how about a freshly baked carrot muffin and tea?"

"I shouldn't. Barry will think I've run away," Jen protested, stepping out of her boots.

"Something you're considering, I gather." Lizzie took her coat and hung it on the clothes tree.

"One more snow day, and I might. My floors are patterned with boot marks, Ian's developed a perpetual whine, and my mother constantly reminds me that Barry could have chosen to work out of the Miami office." Pulling off a beret of soft mohair wool, she gestured at her hair, which was practically throwing sparks into the dry air. "And as if all that isn't enough to push me over the edge, I have a bad case of hat-hair!" She followed Lizzie into the living room. "We're going to be formal?"

"Unless you want to join the little guys in the den. Angelica has every surface in the kitchen covered with baking tins, so we can't sit in there. Stay here and warm up. I'll fix tea."

Jen curled into a corner of the sofa. Behind the fireplace screen the logs glowed neon orange, the charring wood snapping and spitting occasional sparks. The chattering of children in the den was far enough away to be comforting.

"Ian was okay?" Jen asked when Lizzie returned carrying a tray with cups and saucers, teapot, linen napkins, and a plate of muffins. "I hated to dump him on you with Will here, but I had to go to that wake, and Barry. . .well, to hear him tell it, you'd think he had double pneumonia."

"Ian's fine, and we both know that men with head colds are too irritable to baby-sit."

"That's for sure." She watched as Lizzie poured a golden stream of tea into one of the fragile china cups. "When's the ski team due back?"

Lizzie smiled. Sam Kaufman and Steven had taken Sam's boys, Hugh, and Hugh's friend Michael to the Poconos on a skiing trip to celebrate Hugh's tenth birthday. "Not for another hour or two." She tested the tea with a small sip. "You haven't said anything about finally meeting Steven. What'd you think? The truth, now."

Jen set her cup down and took one of the muffins. "Right. I wish I'd known you had tickets to Friday's concert—we could have had dinner together."

"I never thought to mention it. But tell me, did you like him?"

"We only talked for a couple of minutes. You can hardly expect me to know the guy, when all we said was, 'Hello, so happy to meet you.' Now, can you?"

"Jen. . . ."

"Okay. Yes, he seemed very nice."

Lizzie made a face. "Nice? I hate that word. That's it? Nice?"

"Well, I. . .Bo was. . .so distinguished and. . . ."

"And Steven isn't."

"No—yes. . .that isn't what I mean." She brushed her hair back. "I'm sure he's great, Liz. Look at you, you're a different person— that's what counts."

"Yes, yes it is." Lizzie broke off a piece of muffin and studied it. "I'm not trying to repeat Bo. That. . .isn't what I'm doing."

"God, Liz, I didn't mean—"

"I know," Lizzie said, cutting her off.

"But he's married. Doesn't that worry you? As in, where can you go from here?"

"Go? I'm—we're—where we want to be. Why would I want to go anywhere? I have the boys, a comfortable home, a job I love. . .really, sometimes you surprise me."

"No. You're the one pulling the surprises these days. You're going to date this man, take care of one another's children, until. . . ? What if he gets tired of hanging around? What sort of future are you looking at?" She leaned forward and reached for the tray, casting Liz a wicked grin. "And because you fail to make good sense, I get the last muffin."

20

DIVORCE

"Do you like Steve, Mom?" Hugh, lying on his back on his bed, asked this while bouncing a small hard rubber ball off his bedroom wall.

Lizzie closed a drawer on freshly laundered underwear. "Hugh," she warned.

"Okay, but do you?" He pocketed the ball and put the ankle of one leg on the propped knee of the other, swinging his dangling foot up and down, back and forth.

"Yes, I do. How about you?"

"Yeah, he's okay." He studied the movements of his foot. "He gave me his pager number."

"Oh? Why was that?"

Hugh pointed to the ankle that was held aloft. "After I

sprained my ankle—he said I could page him in an emergency. Sort of like insurance, you know?"

"Umm, well, make sure it's a real emergency."

"How come you went over to his house?"

Lizzie, on her way out the door, stopped.

"You know, the other night. Angelica said you were at Steve's."

She nodded. "Oh, yes. . .that's right, I was." She continued through the door. "Don't forget to do your homework before you come down to watch television."

Shivering in the unheated car, Lizzie hugged her coat closer to her body. "Hugh asked me why I was at your house Friday night."

Steve laughed. "Aha! He's found you out." He started the motor. "And what did you say?"

She dug her chin into the warm lining. "Nothing. I didn't know what to say."

"I can imagine."

"He's ten going on thirty, I sometimes think."

"Yeah, it won't take him long to figure out what's what." He glanced at her.

She turned her head and looked out the side window as the car rocked down the driveway on the ice.

"Then what?"

"That'll be a long way off," she said faintly.

He caught his lower lip in his teeth and narrowed his eyes as he swung the car to avoid a sudden hill of snow that jutted out into the road. "Maybe. Does Angelica know your plans this evening?"

"No. Why?"

He smiled. "After dinner we can stop by my place without fear of being tracked down." He reached over and rubbed the back of her neck.

He took her through the garage into the mudroom and on to the kitchen. Recessed lights cast an eerie glow in the gleaming, but stark room. It was quiet, their breathing and the hum of the refrigerator the only sounds. Lizzie leaned against the granite top of the counter and waited while he checked his messages.

"One call," he said.

"It's okay."

His arm around her shoulders, they walked across the kitchen into the darkness of the family room.

"Don't go away," he said, unzipping her parka and slipping it off her shoulders.

She waited while he made his call, listening to his quiet responses to the worried voice she could hear on the other end of the line. After he'd finished, he knelt in front of the fireplace and spent a few minutes starting a fire. Shifting his weight back onto his heels, he watched until the kindling spread flames to the logs. When he stood up, she went to him, and he gathered her in. His body, no longer unfamiliar, was home to hers. They found the couch and undressed in the light and warmth of the fire.

"Lizzie," he whispered, "how much of a commitment can you make?"

She shook her head. "Not now. . .not tonight."

After they made love, they lay quietly for a time. In his arms, his chest pressed so tightly to hers that she could count his heart beats, she tried to push his question—and all it asked of her—away. The logs in the fireplace threw off bursts of flying sparks that reflected on the ceiling and crackled noisily, but it was all show and little warmth, and she was grateful for the afghan they'd pulled over themselves.

Propping himself up on one elbow, he gazed down at her. "Here's my plan. We'll get you a bicycle, and at night, after the boys are asleep, you'll sneak out to the garage, get on it, and pedal like mad here. We'll make love, then you'll pedal home. Under cover of night, just like the French Resistance."

"Why can't I drive over in the car?"

"Noise, lights, not at all romantic."

She smiled. "Steven, you're a nut."

He lay back down and held her. "I'm getting a divorce." He listened to the silence, then said, "Okay. Time to return you to parenthood," and eased his arm from under her shoulders.

A log burst into embers in the fireplace. Lizzie stared up at him, his face profiled against the fading light of the fire. "I'm sorry. You took me by surprise. . .I don't know what to say."

He leaned down and kissed her softly on the lips. "You don't need to say anything. I thought you should know."

21

ELISA

B<small>Y</small> TEN IN THE MORNING THE MEDICAL OFFICE of Drs. Marini, Heller, and Kaufman was usually running smoothly. The women responsible for this could pause to draw a few deep breaths and finally enjoy their morning coffee.

Ellen Haggerty, in charge of making sense out of the multiple insurance claims and companies the office dealt with, nodded toward Sam Kaufman's back as he disappeared into Examining Room 4.

"I'd say his vacation did him a world of good. He's been cheerful as a jay bird ever since he got back from St. Thomas." She gathered up a stack of yellow file folders and tapped their edges with a sharp snap on the counter that skirted the waiting room.

Tammy Decker swung away from her computer screen, where

she was checking on the afternoon appointments. "Thank God one of them's in good spirits," she said.

"You're right," Ellen said. "It's bad enough we have to deal with Marini's moods. Now Heller's biting our heads off."

Tammy nodded. "Yeah, what's with him?"

"I'll tell you what *I* think," Annie Poe said, approaching the counter where they were seated. She lowered her voice. "You know Elizabeth Donnely? She used to be his patient, but now she's Dr. Kaufman's? I heard he was seeing her. So maybe they broke up."

"What? Like they were *dating*?" Tammy asked.

Ellen and Annie rolled their eyes. "Well, yeah, or better," Annie said.

"So what gives with his wife?" Tammy leaned forward, shaking back her short dark hair, definitely interested in the way the conversation was going. "I thought he was married."

"Maybe divorced," Annie said. "I know he has a kid, 'cause he's got his picture on his desk."

Ellen shook her head. "Huh-uh, he's *getting* a divorce. I heard him talking to his lawyer about custody rights and—" She broke off at the sight of Carrie Jackson.

"Ladies, there is still work to be done, and I advise you to get to it," Carrie barked. She turned to Annie, her eyes snapping disapproval through wire-framed glasses that balanced half-way down her nose. "I need x-rays for Mr. Krinsky, and see if the results are back on his latest blood work."

Annie started down the hall. "Right away," she called. "Sorry, Carrie. I meant to get them earlier."

Lizzie considered the contents of her closet. She didn't want to go to dinner in the navy pants suit she had worn all day, but what could she wear that would be warm enough, yet not look like Arctic wear? Harry wasn't helping the decision making process, with his barrage of questions.

"When is St. Patrick's Day do you think? Next week? Does everybody have to wear something green? Do we go to school on St. Patrick's Day? We don't have to go to school on that day, do we, Mom?"

"Yes, Harry, you do, but you just had a day off from school, remember? You didn't go on President's Day." She considered a black wool skirt. She could wear her gray cashmere sweater set with it.

"Mom, are you and Steve going to get married?"

She swung around and looked at him. He was lying on his back on her bed, staring up at the ceiling.

"Well, are you, Mom?"

"No, Harry. Dr. Heller already has a family. And please don't dig your heels into the quilt that way."

"Who's his family? Willy's his son, right?"

"Um-hmm." Or maybe a dress would look better than the skirt.

"Is Gramma his wife?"

"Call her Mrs. Heller, honey. She's not your grandmother. No, she's not his wife, she's his mother. Like I'm your mother, and when you get married, your wife will be Mrs. Donnely, too."

Harry, in the process of sitting up, threw himself back down on the bed with a vehement squawk of protest at the idea of having a wife. "But where's Steve's wife?"

"She lives somewhere else, Harry."

"She left him?"

"I don't know about that. Perhaps it was an agreement—to live in different places."

"Then maybe *you* could be his wife." He rolled to the edge of the bed and hung his head over the side.

"No. No, it doesn't work that way. A man can't have two wives, at least not in this country. You stay married until you get a divorce or one of you dies. Like when Daddy died."

He pulled at a loose thread on his shirt cuff. "I wish Steve didn't have her." He sat up suddenly. "What about Willy? She doesn't live with him either. She left Willy, too?"

Lizzie put aside the skirt, sat down on the bed, and gathered Harry to her. "I don't know what happened to Steve's family, honey, why his wife doesn't live with him or with Will."

He threaded an arm around the back of her waist. "You would never leave Hugh and me. . .would you?"

She rested her cheek on his head. "Never. Wild horses couldn't drag me away."

"What about wild tigers?"

"Nope, and not wild rhinoceroses, either." She kissed his cheek, the skin warm and still baby soft to her lips. "Now, go get your book, and I'll read you a chapter before I go out."

She took her time after reading to Harry. Steve had called earlier to say he had a meeting and asked if she minded a late dinner. In the bathroom she washed her face, patting it dry slowly and studying it in the mirror as she rubbed in moisturizer. Where was she going with this relationship? she wondered. Steve was pursuing a divorce, which, she had to admit, scared her. Because?

Because she was afraid he'd begin to think about marriage, and marriage wasn't. . .it just wasn't. He said those words—"I love you"—so easily, making her inability to utter them all the more glaring. She smoothed on foundation, then considered the several different shades of blush before choosing a rosy one and stroking it across her cheekbones, wishing that the soft bristles of the brush could sweep away her anxious thoughts.

They ate at Steven's favorite restaurant, Andacino's, where the northern Italian food was excellent, the lighting soft, and the service friendly but discreet. It was late and there were only a few diners. They followed Mario past empty tables to one near a window where the reflections of flickering candles danced on the glass.

Steven was quiet, his thoughts obviously elsewhere as they had been for the last couple of weeks. Lizzie felt irritation tightening its grip despite her determination to be upbeat and pleasant. "Steven, you look like you're ready to fall over. Did you get any sleep last night?"

"Yes, of course I got some sleep." He ran a hand over his eyes. "Sorry—didn't mean to take your head off."

"Are there problems with the study?"

"No problems. We're finishing our proposal. Once that's submitted, we wait. Why did you think we had problems?"

"Because you've been a little testy. And you're developing a permanent crease between your eyebrows." She reached across the table and touched the bridge of his nose. "Do you feel like talking?"

"I thought we were, but, okay, we can talk. Something in particular?"

She chewed on her lip. Across the room one of the waiters

dropped a glass.

"Lizzie?"

She reached for his hand. It felt so different from Bo's, the ridge of his knuckles four gentle peaks, where Bo's had been sharp and craggy. She loved the feel of it closing around hers as it now was doing, the fingers tucking hers in easily, firmly, never too tight, connecting them. Often he'd rub his thumb slowly across her palm, sending a shiver of desire through her.

"Your divorce—I've been thinking about it. Can you tell me. . . ?" Her voice trailed away.

"Ah, I see. Yes, sure. We've never talked about Elisa, have we?"

She shook her head. A splinter of panic needled her in the pit of her stomach, and she wondered if it was too late to close the door she'd yanked open. "It's just that two weeks ago you said you were getting a divorce, and we haven't spoken of it since. Something seems to be bothering you. If it's the divorce, or discussing the divorce, then. . . ." She raised her eyes and appealed silently to him.

"No, you're right, we need to talk." He held her gaze for a long moment. "I don't know, Lizzie, I don't know what I thought—that I'd never want a real life, never meet a woman I'd want to spend the rest of my days with? I concentrated on Will and on medicine, and that was it, that was my life. That and a lot of guilt." He watched the circles he was making with his glass on the tablecloth. "The divorce itself is moving along with no hitches. Our lawyers are in touch, and they seem to be getting it done."

"And your wife—Elisa? You and she aren't in touch?"

"No."

"So. . .it's not a friendly divorce. Why the guilt?"

"It's a divorce. Friendly doesn't enter into it. And why the guilt?" He shrugged. "I guess that's why you need to know about Elisa."

"You told me way back that you'd been separated for a lot of years. And you have Will. Did she walk out?"

He shook his head. "No, not at all." He paused, gathering his thoughts. "Elisa and I met in college and got married right after my graduation. Probably should have waited, but that's hindsight. I thought she was a free spirit, which is fine when you're young and dating. It turned out to be not so fine when I was in med school and working my ass off. We were moving toward thirty, but Elisa wasn't having any of it." He looked over Lizzie's shoulder and nodded. "We'd better order. I think they want to close the kitchen."

"She wasn't in med school?" Lizzie asked when the waiter had left with their orders.

"Oh, no. She never finished college. She worked in a boutique that a friend of hers had opened in the Village. Some days she'd get up and spend the day at the store. Some days she wouldn't." He smiled a bitter half smile. "I was studying medicine, such a smart guy, that was me. But I missed diagnosing the case right under my nose."

"She was sick?"

"Very. I got home one morning after a twenty-four hour shift. I was doing my residency. I was dead on my feet most of the time. Lucky to keep myself in motion, so I'm afraid I wasn't taking a lot of notice of what Elisa was about. That morning all I could think about was falling into bed. I unlocked the door to our apartment and walked in. It was dark, completely dark. Outside the sun was shining. Inside. . .nothing. A cave. I mean *no* light was entering, not a ray."

"What was it?"

"Black paint. She'd painted all the windows. And no lights. The lamp cords were unplugged. Every outlet was covered with masking tape. Same with the faucets and drains, all taped up. The phone wire was cut." He finished his drink. "She'd had a complete break with reality. The CIA, the FBI, the police—everyone was spying on her, but it was okay, she assured me, she was in touch with special forces who would get us safely out of the country."

"Oh, God, Steven. . .how awful. But you had no warning? I mean, had she been okay up 'til then?"

He spread his hands. "No hallucinations. But Elisa was what I guess you'd call different. Sam called her whippy, but for me it was part of her charm. She looked at life from an angle none of the rest of us ever considered. So when she was in one of her moods—well, I thought she was more sensitive than the next person, so I'd hunker down and wait until she got over whatever was bothering her." He chewed on his lower lip and was quiet.

"God, Steven."

"I should have realized it was more than that."

Over dinner he told her about the psychiatrists, the in-and-out-and-in-again trips to emergency rooms and psych wards.

"How'd you manage?"

He shook his head. "I don't know. I don't think I saw daylight until Sam and I set up our practice."

"Will?" she asked.

"Eight years ago Elisa had what seemed to be a remission, a cure—I don't know what we thought it was. It was as though she'd come back from a long trip. She went off her meds, and it still continued. We bought the house, and she spent months decorating it. After she got tired of that, she wanted a baby."

Lizzie raised her eyebrows.

"I know, I know. I should have recognized she was substituting one obsession for another, but I thought—well, I don't know what I was thinking."

They ordered coffee. Mario's dark eyes were sadder than usual as he surveyed their unfinished dinners, and they assured him that the food had been delicious, that it was their appetites that were poor.

"Elisa's heart was set on the perfect baby," he continued after Mario had brought the coffee. "The delivery—" He shook his head. "It seemed to go on forever. It was grim. And Will—they had to work for over an hour on him. Then he was rushed to the neonatal ward and zonked into one of their units, wires and tubes everywhere. She refused to see him." He ran a hand over his face. Lizzie saw tears gathering in his eyes. "She's never seen him.

"She has a brother in Connecticut. Jack. He took Elisa, I took Will. . .and that's been it. At first I'd go up to see her. She was hospitalized for nearly a year after Will was born. Usually she refused to see me, and, finally, we—Jack and I—decided it was best if I stayed away."

Lizzie looked away from the pain in his eyes. "Steven, I'm so sorry."

He nodded. "Yeah, I know. I hate to talk about it. Like death."

"What about now? Is she any better?"

"No, not really. Death is not a bad analogy. She's never gone back to being Elisa. Now she's sort of robot-like." He shook his head. "That's wrong, I don't mean she's like a robot, but she's drained—do you know what I mean? Like the essence of her is gone."

"What does she do?"

"Not much. She lives with Jack—he never married—and there's a housekeeper. Periodically she screws around with her medication and ends up in the hospital." He closed his eyes for a moment.

"And Will, what does he know?"

Steve nodded. "He knows she's sick. When he's a little older, we'll talk about the sickness. It scares the hell out of me." He cleared his throat. "I'm sorry—did you want dessert?"

She shook her head. "Let's just leave."

The cold air shocked their lungs, but Lizzie, taking his arm, said, "I think we're breathing again."

22

AUNT PAM

"GO AWAY! I CAN DO IT MYSELF!" Harry's shouts, accompanied by Mickey's frantic barking, reached Steve as he turned into the Donnelys' driveway. Curious and a little concerned, he headed for the far side of the house, where he saw a boy standing under one of the tall pine trees at the edge of the property. Mickey was bouncing around the kid's feet and leaping at the trunk as high as his short legs allowed. As Steve got closer he could see that he had been fooled by the slim build and short haircut. It was a young woman who stood there wearing jeans and a black sweatshirt, looking like a teenager.

Lizzie had called earlier in the week to tell him that her sister would be spending a few days with her. In New York on business, it seemed Pam had some time before she had to return to

California. With auburn hair and a smattering of freckles across high cheekbones and over the bridge of her nose, she bore little resemblance to Lizzie.

"Go on, Aunt Pam, go away!" Harry yelled from high over their heads.

"You must be Steve." She had a husky voice and Hugh's and Lizzie's grin.

"And you're Aunt Pam. Having trouble?" He looked up through thick branches at a pair of dangling legs, which he presumed belonged to Harry.

"'Fraid so. I have a nephew stuck up in this tree."

"I'm not stuck! Tell her, Steve, tell her I can get down myself."

He peered at Harry, who was further from the ground than he himself would ever want to be. "How you doing up there, Harry?"

"Good, Steve. I'm practicing my climbing."

"Yep. I can see that." He exchanged a worried look with Pam.

"Maybe you could ask Liz for a ladder," Pam whispered.

"Well, let's think a minute. I'd hate to worry her. You and I can probably worry enough for all of us."

"You have a point there." She studied him, her eyes a deep blue. "What'll we do?"

He peered through the branches, held out from the trunk like widespread arms although far from welcoming. "I could probably get to the fourth or fifth branch. After that, I think vertigo might do me in."

She giggled. "That or your weight."

"Okay, point taken." He handed her his jacket.

"Oh, no, don't do this!" she cried. Mickey circled their feet, his wagging tail advertising *his* approval of the situation. "How about the fire department? They rescue kittens—I'm sure they'd rescue a little boy."

"Do you have your rope up there, Harry?" Steve called, ignoring the suggestion.

Harry didn't respond immediately. When he did, his voice was faint. "I forgot a rope. Should I have one?"

"Well, that's okay, but you know what you could use?"

"What, Steve?"

"A sherpa."

Silence again descended before Harry yelled, "I don't have that either. What is it?"

"I was afraid you forgot your sherpa. It's a native guide. Mountain climbers always use them." He stressed the word 'always.'

"Oh."

"I think I'll be your sherpa today." Steve pulled himself up to the first branch.

"Oh, Lord!" Pam peered up at him. "Now I'll have two broken bodies to explain to Liz. Are you sure this is wise?"

"I'm positive it isn't. You're looking at the kid who wouldn't even go near a jungle gym." He managed to hoist himself up a few more branches. "Okay, come down to this branch," Steve directed, indicating the one slapping its needles in his face.

"This is fun, right, Steve?"

"Harry, I haven't had this much fun in ages."

Together they made a slow descent, Harry moving nimbly above a scuffling, huffing Steve.

Pam met them, her eyes level with Steve's shoes, her expression a mixture of relief and exasperation. "Look at you two—pine needles all over you, clothes ripped—we're all three going to be in trouble."

"No, we won't, Aunt Pam. Mom says I need practice before I climb a mountain. And anyway, Steve's a sherpa." He waited until Steve had both feet on the ground, then put grimy hands on his shoulders and swung down from the bottom branch.

"Let's not mention the sherpa business to your mother, Harry. And don't climb this tree again."

Harry looked surprised. "But I climb it all the time—it's my practice tree." He jogged off toward the back of the house, whistling between his teeth, Mickey at his heels.

Pam avoided Steve's eyes. "I didn't know—honest to God," she said. "Listen, let's go sit on the porch and start all over. I'm really not as troublesome as you must think I am."

Steve put his hand out for his jacket. "Your sister will be wondering where we are. But, okay—it'll give me a chance to catch my breath." They walked across the grass, avoiding the yellow and purple cups of emerging crocus, and climbed the steps to the front porch.

Sitting down on the swing, she said, "Liz is fixing dinner for the kids. She won't miss us."

He took the wicker chair opposite her, and they regarded one another for a moment or two.

"So you and Lizzie are. . .what? Dating?"

Steve nodded. "Yes, we are. Are you going to inquire about my intentions?"

Pam laughed. "I wasn't going to, but you can tell me. And, oh, yes, don't forget your prospects."

Mickey bounded up the porch steps and jumped onto Steve's lap. "I guess dog hair can't hurt, what with the pine tar and needles," he said.

"Liz seems to be doing okay. Joking aside, I'm glad she has you for. . .a friend?"

"Yeah, I think we're friends."

"She's afraid I'll give you a hard time, you know. I guess going back to the days when Bo and I squared off."

"Ah. And are you? Going to give me a hard time?"

She glanced at him, then turned her attention to Mickey, reaching across to rub his ears. Her hands were square and finely boned and seemed to find the spots that Mickey enjoyed best. "Aren't you at all curious why Bo and I didn't get along?"

"Okay, I'll bite. Why didn't you get along with Bo?"

"I don't get along with bastards."

Steve's eyes widened. He waited while a car minus its muffler roared past the house. "You think Lizzie was married to a bastard?"

"Without a doubt." She pushed with her foot to set the swing in motion.

Steve regarded her for a long moment. "I don't think I want to go there."

Pam raised her eyebrows. "You'd make a terrible lawyer."

"Probably. From what I understand, your family is already full of them."

"Including Bo."

He sighed. "I see."

"That I'm determined to talk about the late, great senator?"

"Why is that?"

"Because I bet Lizzie never talks about him. Am I right? And I think—if you're serious about her, which you seem to be—that you should know what fifteen years of living with him have done to her."

"Come on, Pam," Steve said, setting Mickey down and rising. "Before we do square off, let's go in and see if Lizzie's ready."

"So I see you two have met," Lizzie said when they walked into the kitchen, where she and Angelica were studying a pan of lasagne. "Let's give it another fifteen minutes, Angelica."

"Yes. It needs to be making the bubbles." Angelica took the pot holders from Liz and put the pan into the oven.

"Another fifteen minutes?" Hugh, sitting at the kitchen table, put his head down on his outstretched arms and moaned. "I'm totally starving!"

"Well, I'm afraid you'll have to totally wait," Liz said, giving his hair a tousle as she passed him. "Steven, did I ever tell you that some of your ideas are absolutely brilliant? Taking Pam and me out to dinner is one of the best." She looked closely at him. "You've got something on your—*look* at this." She touched the front of his shirt, where there was a smear of pine tar on the button placket. "And you have pine needles in your hair." She gave him a questioning look.

"Tell me, Liz," Pam said, putting her arm around her sister and heading her out of the kitchen. "Do you know what a sherpa is?"

23

BLOOD

SPRING HAD TAKEN A STEP OR TWO BACKWARD, and Lizzie lamented the loss of its April promise, so real only yesterday. The drop in temperature and the accompanying storm that had swept in during the day were predicted to extend over the entire weekend. She watched dark rivulets of rain snake down the kitchen window as she washed up the pots and dishes she'd used to prepare the lemon chicken, warming in the oven.

She felt sorry for Hugh. He had planned a party for Harry for the evening, working hard on whom to invite, the menu, even what to wear. The weather precluded the backyard treasure hunt, and three of the boys hadn't arrived, including Will. She knew that Steven had planned on going to Queens to get him; she also knew that traffic into and out of the city was probably impossible.

In the den five little boys were consuming hot dogs and soda with Hugh watching over them. He had insisted on handling every aspect of the party, so she resisted the urge to check on them. She wished Steven would call. It was already past seven; the party had begun at five-thirty.

Hugh burst into the kitchen. "More food, Mom. Those guys are still hungry! And I think someone's coming. I heard a car in the driveway."

"Check and see, will you, Hugh?"

"It's Steve and Will," he called on his way back to the den.

"I'm here, Elizabeth! At last!" Will tottered into the kitchen, struggling out of his jacket.

"At last indeed, but at least you made it." Lizzie helped him out of the jacket. "Where's your dad?"

"He had to get his doctor bag, 'cause he banged his finger."

"Oh, my, that's too bad. The boys are in the den, Will."

"Okay! I'm going to the party!"

She followed him with a bowl of popcorn and a plate of grilled hot dogs. Returning to the kitchen, she found Steven at the sink. "I was afraid you weren't going to make it. Awful weather, hmm?" She kissed his cheek, finding it wet and cold. "Steven?" She put a hand on his head. "You're soaked."

"Yeah, I had to change a tire. Cut my thumb. Open my bag, would you, Lizzie?"

"Change a tire? In the rain?"

"Stupid, I know—can you open the bag? It's there on the table."

But, noticing the sink, Lizzie had stepped back, shocked by the vividness of large splatters of red blood against white porcelain. She saw that he was holding a bloody handkerchief around the base of his thumb.

"My God, Steven, what—"

"Get the bag. . .*please*, Lizzie."

She brought it over to the sink. "I'll drive you to the hospital. You must need stitches. . .there's so much blood."

"Probably, but I didn't hit an artery—I think I can take care of it. You can help."

"Oh, no! I faint at the sight of blood."

"That's okay, you can faint later. There should be a pair of scissors sealed in paper in that side pocket. Take them out, and do you see the gauze? That's it. You're going to cut three thick squares, but you have to be careful with it. Spread that paper. . .yeah, that one. Spread it out and set the gauze on it."

"Where did you get the flat?" she asked as she worked.

"Coming back on the approach to the bridge, the G.W."

"Oh, Steven." She winced. "Why didn't you call Triple-A?"

"We'd have been there all night," he said as she set the last piece of gauze on the paper.

"How's this?"

"Good. Next we need antiseptic. There should be a small bottle of it—that's it."

"I'm going to remove the handkerchief," he explained. "As soon as I do, you pour that whole bottle on the cut."

Cap unscrewed, she held the bottle over the sink, but her vision jiggled dangerously when he removed the blood- soaked handkerchief and she saw the deep gash that cut diagonally across the fleshy base of his thumb.

"Pour!"

She poured, glanced at him, then away. "I'm sorry," she whispered.

He exhaled sharply, half laugh, half groan. Quickly pressing the squares of gauze over the cut, he said, "You're doing just fine. We're ready to suture."

She caught her breath. "No! I can't—"

"I'm kidding. Look in the bag and find a packet marked 'butterflies'. . .that's it. Take one out and peel the paper off one side. We're going to place it on the cut together. Hold it there. . .yeah, that's it. . .press down. . .a little firmer. . .okay. That does it."

Lizzie stared at his hand. The center of the bandage was turning crimson. "It's still bleeding."

With his left hand he turned on the faucet and reached for the sponge that rested on the back ledge of the sink. She took it from him. "I'll clean up. Let me drive you to the hospital."

"It'll take a few minutes, but it's going to clot."

"All right. At least sit down." She sprayed and wiped the sink. Squeezing the sponge, she watched the last drops of blood run out of its blue pores. From a cabinet under the counter she produced a bottle of Scotch, poured half a tumblerful and took it over to the table where he sat watching her, his elbow resting in front of him, his hand in the air.

"Thank you." He took several swallows before setting the glass down. "You're angry."

She sat down across from him. A flash of lightning brightened the room, and the lights flickered. She waited for the low grumble of thunder. Biz scuttled into the room and crawled under the table, his nails scraping the tile floor. "No," she said, shaking her head slowly.

He moved his shoulders in a questioning shrug. "What, then?"

She was quiet for a long moment. "There are people who

depend on you, Steven, people who care deeply for you. You have to start taking better care of yourself. You have to get more sleep, wear your overcoat—and stop changing tires on the George Washington Bridge. God, Steven, you could have been killed."

He gazed at her. "Care deeply for me. Is that the best you can do, Lizzie?"

She didn't respond, and the silence grew. In the den delighted shouts of little boys were followed by peals of laughter.

Later, when the children were in bed—she insisted that he leave Will to spend the night with Harry, he made coffee while she retrieved the dishes Hugh had overlooked in the den. He found her there, holding an empty popcorn bowl, looking out at the rain. He put his hands on her shoulders.

"Do you think I'm an emotional cripple?"

Her voice was so quiet that at first he thought he had misunderstood. "Do I...? No, of course not. I think you've taken a couple hard hits, but a cripple? No." He said the last word firmly and bent his head to look at her face, but she turned away.

"No," she repeated, shaking her head. "I used to think that time, a couple of years, would cure me. Now, I wonder."

24

SEDER

"YOU'RE SURE YOU'RE OKAY WITH THIS?" Steve asked as they circled the marble fountain at the bottom of the 72nd Street off ramp of the West Side Highway. "It's not too late to call and say we're not coming." He glanced at Lizzie. She'd been quiet for most of the ride in from Jersey, in profile her posture a little too straight, her expression unfocused. When they were stuck in thick, slow-moving bridge traffic, he'd reached for her hand and rubbing the back of it with his thumb, felt the rigidity of her bones through the pliant leather of her glove. "Seriously, it's no big deal to cancel."

"What if they hate me?"

"Doubtful. More likely you'll hate them. They can be . . . 'overwhelming' is probably the best word to describe the Hellers."

A couple of weeks before he'd had a phone call from his cousin

Debbie, reminding him of the seder that was to be in her and her husband Dan's West Side apartment instead of at her parents' house on Long Island, where the family usually convened. She'd added to her invitation, "If there's someone you'd like to bring, that'd be okay, Steve."

"Someone I'd like to bring? I hadn't thought of that. Thanks, Deb," he'd said. "Maybe I will. Bring someone."

He made a point of getting to the first night seder each year, one of the few times he saw his relatives. More important was having Will see him in their midst. He was always conscious of Will's aloneness—no mother, no brothers or sisters, and a father only on weekends—and always wanting to fix it for his child. He despaired that Will, a "special child" in the language of the education system, would spend his adulthood on an analyst's couch, dealing with the aftermath of a deprived childhood.

But until Debbie mentioned bringing someone, he hadn't considered inviting Lizzie. Other than his parents no one in the family had met her; heard of her, he was sure, for his mother would surely have mentioned her to family members. But now he realized he hadn't given Lizzie's attendance the deliberation it deserved. What was he thinking, throwing her into the lions' den?—an appropriately Biblical metaphor.

He held her hand in the elevator. He loved her, and here he was, placing her in the cross hairs of his relatives' curious stares. Conversation would halt, and Lizzie and he would stand there in the deafening silence, deer caught in headlights. And then she'd have to endure a lengthy and foreign ritual. Jeezus, what an idiot he'd been! He reached out to stop the elevator, when she loosened her hand from his grip and slipped an arm around his waist.

"Don't worry. I've faced rooms full of pissed off Republican women," she murmured. "How bad can this be? Anyhow, your family's going to love me." She turned to him with what he thought of as Hugh's mischievous grin, and they started to laugh.

They got off the elevator, still laughing, to find standing at the open door to her apartment, Cousin Debbie— fiftyish, broad-beamed, and a smile on her face that stretched from ear to ear. Steve, keeping a protective arm around Lizzie, kissed Debbie and apologized for being late.

"He's always late," she told Lizzie, "but he's my favorite cousin, so I can't get angry with him. I'm Debbie Cohen, and Dan and I are so happy that you're joining us."

"Elizabeth Donnely, and thanks for including me. That was nervous laughter you heard. We're both a little edgy about my being here."

Before Debbie could reply, Will rocketed into the foyer, trailing cousins. "Elizabeth! Daddy!" Debbie grinned at Steve and said something about forgetting edginess, but he could barely hear her in the wave of kids' chatter and family greetings.

There were some stares, but overall it proved to be a bearable, even enjoyable evening. An eagerness to meet and monopolize Lizzie prevailed right through the long dinner. Suddenly everyone was an expert on Jewish history and tradition, hell bent on educating the lone Christian in the room, and Lizzie the teacher made an excellent pupil.

By the time dinner had ended, she saw that Will, sitting at her side, was struggling to stay awake. Chairs groaned as their occupants, filled with Debbie's excellent brisket and all that had accompanied it, pushed away from a table littered with matzo crumbs and dishes.

"Stevie! I have to talk to you! Come with me." His great aunt, known to the family as Old Aunt Ruti to distinguish her from her daughter, who at the age of seventy-one was called Young Aunt Ruti, had issued the command in a croaking voice as they were leaving the table.

"Mother, we have to go," Young Aunt Ruti said. "It's late, and we have a long ride ahead of us."

"We'll go, we'll go. First I have to talk to this boy. Maybe he knows what it is I need to take to get rid of this cough. All winter I've had it." She wheezed and gasped as she stumped toward an alcove off the living room, leaning heavily on her cane.

Steve looked over his shoulder at Debbie and mouthed, "Help!" before following the old woman.

"Now, Stevie, you're the smart doctor, I know that, but it's time you found yourself a nice Jewish girl and settled down." Old Aunt Ruti had trouble hearing, but worse, thinking everyone else did, she spoke in a voice that easily over-powered nearby conversations and commandeered attention. "Get married! Get a mother for that boy of yours. A nice Jewish girl, you hear me?"

He watched Debbie enlisting Lizzie's help in carrying dishes into the kitchen before turning to the old woman and steering the conversation to her physical complaints, which he knew were man-ifold. When he'd finally convinced her to listen to her daughter about leaving, he rounded up Will for his parents and went to find Lizzie. He was eager to leave.

He hadn't realized just how tense he'd been until they were in the car, the dinner behind them, the April night air surrounding them, dark and cold.

"I think they really did like me." Lizzie rocked a little in the passenger seat in an attempt to get warm.

"Of course they did. I was afraid Will was going to become permanently attached to your side."

"I wonder. . . ."

"What do you wonder?"

"If that's such a good thing."

He grinned. "Well, no. I wouldn't want to see a permanent attachment," he said lightly. "That would present all sorts of problems."

"Maybe you should."

"Maybe I should? What?"

"Find a nice Jewish girl."

He glanced at her, but couldn't make out her expression in the dark. "You're kidding, right?" When she didn't reply, he felt exasperation grip him, the kind he felt when he was tired and Will kicked up a storm. "Lizzie, she's an old lady who gives that talk to all her grandchildren and grandnieces and nephews. I thought we'd have a good laugh about it." He hit the horn as a cab cut him off. "Idiot!"

They rode in silence for awhile. "Come on, Lizzie," he finally said, "don't do this."

"It never occurred to me. The idea that maybe I'm keeping you from getting on with your life. I mean, maybe you'd like to. . .well, you know, have a family again. And there's Will. He is becoming attached to me, and how fair is that to him?"

"Okay, great. What do you suggest?" When she didn't answer, he said, "Drop you off on Stelfox Street? Say so long, it's been nice, but now I'm off to find a nice Jewish girl I'll immediately fall in love with and marry? That makes a lot of sense."

"I don't know." He could barely hear her over the traffic noise.

They didn't speak for the rest of the ride to Aspenhill. Once in her driveway, he set the brake, cut the motor, and gazed at her for a moment before getting out. On the porch he took her arm and pulled her down beside him on the swing. The street was quiet, but the wind, cold for April, swept noisily through the trees. Branches just beginning to leaf out swept nervously here and there, making strange, moving shadows on their faces. Somewhere a cat demanded a mate in yowling tones. He held both her hands.

She leaned her head on his shoulder. "Don't say good-bye."

"No. Bad idea. . .very bad idea."

25

SURPRISE

Pausing on the porch on her way into the house late one
afternoon in May, Lizzie dropped her school bag to the floor and
sat for a moment on the swing, relishing the feel of sunlight on her
face. Overhead the trees formed a tentative network of green
against a pale blue sky. In a bed bordering the driveway, prim daf-
fodils and less diffident tulips waved gently in the breeze. Summer
perennials were already thrusting up out of the warmed soil. For
weeks the air, dense with fragrance, had been filling her with
unnamed yearnings, distracting her from the simplest task. She
didn't want to go to work, she didn't want to stay home. The only
thing she *could* identify was the wanting part. A whiff of newly
mowed grass, and her day was thrown out of alignment. Thirty-
seven years old and felled by a teenage case of spring fever, she

thought.

Thanks to Stuart Parker, she had been delayed at school and was late getting home. Stuart had found it amusing to phone 911 on his cell phone and report a nonexistent fire in the school basement. It had taken hours to sort the whole thing out. She inhaled one last intoxicating breath and reluctantly went inside.

In the kitchen she found Harry arranging soda crackers and slices of American cheese on a plate.

"It's a. . .what did you call it, Angelica?"

"Is the appetizer, Harry."

"Yeah, that."

"May I sample one?" Lizzie asked.

"Sure."

She chewed the cracker as she watched him at work. "Umm, delicious. Who are you fixing them for?" With his lower lip caught between his teeth, Harry was focusing his full attention on alternating cheese with cracker and didn't answer. She peered over Angelica's shoulder into a large pot. "Baked beans?"

"Is what Hugh and Harry said, Liz."

"With hot dogs cut up in them," Harry added.

Upstairs she found Hugh at the desk in his room. A tumble of auburn hair threatened to cut off his sight as he bent over several sheets of paper. "Homework?" she asked, leaning over and pushing the hair off his forehead before kissing it.

"Yeah and I'm almost finished. Just have to put my book report in this thing I got for it." He held up a red folder.

She looked at the read-out on the clock radio. "And it's only five-thirty. You're ahead of schedule, aren't you?"

"Uh-huh." He smiled to himself as he arranged the sheets of

white composition paper in the folder.

"Well, that's good, Hugh. Something special planned?"

"Sort of."

"Okay. I guess you'll tell me when the time is right."

He twisted around in his chair and studied her. "You probably want to get ready for dinner. You know, maybe comb your hair and put on some perfume."

She narrowed her eyes and looked at him closely. He was maintaining a sober expression, but the rapid blinking of his eyes reflected excitement. "To eat beans and franks? Or are you planning on taking me out?"

"No, I just, you know, thought you'd want to look real nice."

"Okay, Hugh, I'll lay on the perfume."

When she returned to the first floor, Harry was setting the table in the dining room.

"I see we're having guests," she said, noting two extra place-settings. "Who's eating with us, Harry?" Before he could reply the doorbell rang, and the dogs set up a chorus of barks.

Harry jumped, emitting a high-pitched, nervous giggle. "I got it, I got it," he cried, racing for the hall.

"Harry, slow down," she cautioned, picking up the paper napkins he had spilled at the sound of the bell. She was turning to go to the kitchen when she heard Will's voice, as excited as Harry's. He rushed into the room in his signature gait and hugged her tightly around the waist. She kissed the top of his curls.

"Will, one of my favorite boys. This is such a super surprise."

"Elizabeth, we're here for dinner. Dad brought a pie and, oh, yeah, Gramma said to say hi."

He disappeared into the hall, having barely missed bumping

into Steve.

"This is like a British comedy—characters exiting, characters entering," she said.

He kissed her, leaving her, as always, momentarily disoriented, then placed the pie in her hands.

"Your mother's?"

"Bakery."

"Hey, Steve!" Hugh arrived, breathless, having raced down the steps three at a time.

"Hey, Hugh. All set?" He indicated the living room with a nod of his head.

Lizzie raised her eyebrows in a silent question.

"The boys and I need to talk for a minute," was all he would say. He was humming under his breath, alive with contained energy. And she noticed that he was wearing his favorite tie, a bold blend of primary colors that wasn't too easy on the eye.

"Angelica, what do you imagine those guys are up to?" She set the pie on the kitchen table and chose a few tomatoes from a bowl on the counter.

Angelica shrugged. "You okay to serve dinner, Liz? Maria, she is going to drive us to a movie. Is okay with you?"

"Sure. You enjoy the movie. It looks like I'll have plenty of help."

Harry came in holding out an empty plate. "Mom," he complained, "look what Biz and Mickey did."

"The cheese and crackers?" Lizzie asked, slicing the last tomato.

"Yep, every single one. I guess we won't have. . . whatever."

Dinner was noisy, and Lizzie and Steve did the cleaning up, as she decided it was safer for the well being of the china and the kitchen floor to keep the boys away from both.

"Why are they in the living room?" she asked Steve. "And do you want coffee?"

"They're waiting for us, and yes, please."

"All right, let's go in while the coffee drips. This is beginning to feel like a birthday or Christmas."

"Exactly."

"You keep smiling at me. It's not my birthday."

"I know that. Let's go."

The boys, although seated, looked as though they would be better off racing around in circles. Lizzie could see it in their bright eyes and jittery movements.

She sat down, and Steve took the footstool facing her.

"This better not be another dog," Lizzie warned.

"No!" Harry cried, falling off his chair in giggles. He pulled himself together, muttered, "Sorry," and climbed back onto his seat.

"Lizzie," Steve began, then cleared his throat. "Since Hugh is the man in the family, it was Hugh I spoke with last week-end. We had a long talk, and I told him about my prospects, which are fairly good, and about my character, which is also fairly good."

A warning bell chimed in Lizzie's head, but she couldn't think how to stop him.

"I admitted to not being a very religious man, but he was okay with that." He paused and looked at each of the boys. Their expressions were identical, expressions seen on the faces of an audience watching a magician about ready to perform a favorite trick.

"Lizzie," he said in a hoarse voice. "Lizzie, Hugh's given his permission for me to ask you to marry me." He took both her hands in his. "Will you? Marry me?"

She stared at him and for a moment was afraid the buzzing in her ears meant she would faint. The room was silent but for the ticking of the clock and the loud breathing of Hugh, Harry, and Will. She didn't think Steve was breathing. She knew she wasn't.

She began to shake her head in disbelief at what was happening. He was proposing marriage—in front of their sons!

"It's okay, Mom. It's okay." She realized Harry was saying something, and she turned to look at him.

"It's okay, there's a you-know-what, but Steve—"

"Shut up!" Hugh yelled. "We aren't supposed to say that!"

"—wants to give it to you when you're alone with him," Harry finished in a rush. "Don't worry—you're going to get one. You know what I mean."

Will and Hugh glared at him.

Lizzie tried to relax her fingers, which were icy in Steve's warm grasp. "Steven," she managed, then stopped. Trying again, she said in as firm a voice as she could muster, "Steven, I think we need to have a word."

"Okay. Excuse us, fellows," he said. "Why don't you catch some TV and give Lizzie and me a few minutes."

When they were alone, she said, trying to keep her voice low and in control, "I can't believe this. What were you *thinking*?"

He bit down on his lower lip, which she saw with a stab at her heart was trembling. "I was thinking I love you. I was thinking I want to marry you," he said softly.

"But—in front of the *children*? Why in God's name would you involve *them*?"

"Because they're already involved. It's not just you and me. Their lives will change, too."

"But. . .but what can I say? They'll hate me."

She saw his face recoil as if slapped.

"If you say 'no,' you mean." Steve's voice was very low. "No. We talked about that possibility. They won't hate you. They'll be disappointed, but they won't hate you. I think."

"You *think?* Oh, God. . . ."

He tightened his grip on her hands. "Lizzie, remember what Harry said about believing in Santa Claus? Remember, before Christmas?"

She shook her head, thoroughly confused. "Santa Claus?"

"Harry said he'd use his head, but he'd also trust. I know it's hard for you, because of all you've been through with your dad and Bo. You loved them, and sometimes they failed you. I'll try never to fail you, Lizzie." He held her gaze.

She tried to swallow, but her mouth was dry and her throat felt swollen.

"Look at our hands."

She looked down at their four intertwined hands, hers clutching his, or was it the other way around?

"I need you. I think you need me."

She hesitated, then shook her head. "I don't think I can do this," she whispered.

"You said that once before, and yet you did it, did it really well."

"Can we come in now?" Hugh asked, leaning his head around the doorway.

"Lizzie?"

"Yes, come in, Hugh."

The boys filed in and huddled together on the couch, their exuberance of a few minutes before gone. She looked at each of them, then at Steven.

"I think. . .what I think is we shouldn't rush this. Let's take our time. You know that you've sprung a surprise on me, and," she said, looking at Will and Steven, "Harry and Hugh know I don't handle surprises very well. This is a big decision you're asking me to make, a decision to make for all of us, so please. . .please understand. . .I'm going to need time." In the silence that followed, she was certain she could hear expectations like shiny mylar balloons, deflating all around her, but she didn't know what else to do.

26

BO

"DR. HELLER. . . ." Tammy Decker's voice came over the inter-com. "Sorry to interrupt, but there's a woman out here—claims you'll see her, even though she does *not* have an appointment. I told her you were going to the hospital, but she insists." She lowered her voice. "To tell the truth? She's real pushy."

Steve asked Mrs. Faraldi to excuse him for a moment and picked up the phone. "Does this woman have a name, Tammy?"

"Oh, yeah, sorry. It's Pamela. . .Wart."

"Ward?"

"That's it."

"Ah. All right, put her in my office and tell her I'll be with her in a few minutes. And Tammy. . . ."

"Yes, Dr. Heller?"

"Be nice to Ms. Ward."

"Oh, okay. I'll treat her nice."

"That's it. Thanks."

Turning his attention to Mrs. Faraldi, he was finally able to convince her that there was no reason for her to be admitted to the hospital. After renewing her prescriptions and reviewing the instructions with her, he left the examining room and went down the hall to his office.

He found Pam examining the diplomas and certificates that hung on the wall over a bookcase crammed with journals and textbooks. She looked over her shoulder. "All this learning, and you can't get a simple marriage proposal right."

Steve grinned. Gone were the jeans and sweater. This was Pam the businesswoman in a dark suit that spoke of custom tailoring, pale gray silk blouse, slim leather pumps, and a Coach briefcase, which she had parked on a corner of his desk. "What's up, Pam? Everything okay?"

"In California everything's okay. What the hell is going on in New Jersey?" She dropped into a chair facing his desk and crossed one slender leg over the other.

"You've spoken to Lizzie." He sat down across from her.

"No. I've spoken to Hugh." She breathed out audibly, drama and disgust in every inch of the exhalation. "I love my sister dearly, and I owe her big—for years she ran interference for me with our father. But love and admire her as I do, there are times when she's a horse's ass. Here she has a great guy—" she gave him a wide smile—"offering her all sorts of love and devotion, and what does she do?" Another dramatic sigh. "Turns him down."

Steve raised a warning hand. "Not exactly. She did leave the door open a few inches. But let's talk about you. Are you here on business, or is this pleasure?"

She gave him an impatient look. "I came to see *you*. I figure I can return some of what I owe Liz by giving you family support."

"So, all the way from California to hold my hand. I call that a damn good sister." He rocked back in his chair. "When you could have just called."

"Nope. I'm here to take you to lunch."

Steve laughed. "Okay, that sounds good. I guess I have to eat." He glanced at his watch. "My problem is I have to be at the hospital at one."

"Let the guy lie on the table a few extra minutes. Take a couple bucks off your fee. What we need is lunch."

"Okay, here's what we can do. If you don't mind eating in the hospital cafeteria, I can check in, and they can call me when my patient gets there. That may give us time for a bowl of chili. What do you say?"

Pam shrugged. "Sounds like I'm getting off with a cheap lunch. Sure, let's go."

At the hospital they worked their way through the cafeteria line and settled at a table in a far corner, isolated from most of the other diners.

Dr. Gordon, six-five-two. . .Dr. Charles Gordon, six-five-two.

"You'd think they'd turn that thing off in here and give you guys a moment's peace." Pam took her dishes off the tray and set it aside.

"You get used to it." He slid his tray onto the table and set her briefcase on an empty chair. "You eat like that, you're going to have clogged arteries by the time you're forty," he said, eyeing Pam's roast beef, mashed potatoes with gravy, and large bowl of chocolate ice cream.

"Oh, boy. Maybe I'd better rethink the object of this visit. What I don't need is a nag in the family."

Steve peeled the foil from a packet of dressing and drizzled its contents on his salad. "What sort of support did you come two thousand miles to give me?"

"You know, if you'd listened to me back in March, maybe none of this would be necessary."

Steve paused, his fork half way to his mouth, and regarded her across the table. "It's the Bo thing again, isn't it?"

"It's got to be the Bo thing. There's no getting around it."

"I don't see how reciting Bo's faults is going to help me change Lizzie's mind."

"I know you don't and that's what I'm here to explain, that is, if you'll let me."

Steve began to eat again.

"I'm going to assume by your silence that you'll at least listen. You see, this goes way back to Liz and Bo and how they ended up married." She stabbed a piece of beef with her fork.

"This makes me very uncomfortable, I have to tell you. Every marriage has its ups and downs. If Lizzie wanted me to know about her life with Bo, she'd tell me."

Pam exhaled in disbelief. "Oh, right, the queen of stoicism is going to share. Not likely. Believe me, Liz, number one, detests self-pity, and, number two, guards her privacy like a mother tiger. Now, listen to me for ten minutes."

"When Bo got out of law school, he clerked for my uncle, who's chief justice of the Pennsylvania Supreme Court. He—"

"Really?"

"My uncle? Oh, yeah, we have judges all over the place. Anyhow, Uncle Frank introduced Bo to Dad, whose firm was looking for bright young associates. With Dad and Bo, it was love at first sight. They were like identical twins separated at birth. I think Bo was dearer to Dad than either of his daughters." She paused, narrowed her eyes and stared beyond Steve as she thought about what she'd just said before shaking off the momentary reverie. "Want some of this cole slaw?"

"No, thanks."

"I guess, early on, Dad decided Bo was the perfect man for Liz, who at the time was at Smith, majoring in education—which infuriated him. She was supposed to be his lawyer child, and he felt it was pure defiance on her part that she refused to consider law school. In Bo he saw the answer, is what I figure. He'd kill two birds with one stone: Bo would be his son, and Liz would learn to mend her ways."

"And it didn't happen."

"Well, we know the first part did, but, no, Liz stood her ground. Which was really remarkable, given Bo's special powers of persuasion."

"Wait." Steve put up a hand as if to ward off a blow. "Give me a minute. What's that mean exactly, 'powers of persuasion?' Is this code? Are you saying he was physically abusive?" He had to work hard to get the last two words out.

Pam shook her head. "I don't think so."

Dr. Heller, four-oh-one. . .Dr. Steven Heller, four-oh-one.

"I'll be right back." He walked over to a wall phone. When he returned, he said, "It's okay. We have some time."

"Good. To answer your question, no, I never figured Bo was into the physical power trip. I do know there was a thing with the kids. Hugh ended up in the emergency ward, which I found out was Bo's doing, the bastard.

"No, what Bo was into was control and mind games. He was a master of the English language. Listen to tapes of his speeches sometime. They're brilliant. Where he really excelled was debating. I don't think he ever lost a debate, which made him a politician to reckon with." She waved her ice cream spoon. "The thing was, Bo could attack or humiliate with a few chosen words. My take on it is that Liz never knew when those words would fly. He'd be charming one minute and your worst nightmare the next. In the beginning, though, he was all charm, and I think Liz figured by marrying him, she'd finally be free of Dad."

"Which never works."

"True. But when you're twenty-one, you think it will. Anyhow, I think both of them were seeing through the proverbial rose-colored glasses when they looked at each other. And Bo had to spend fifteen years trying to reconfigure Liz into what he thought she should be. That's one point where his and Dad's ideas diverged, because Bo didn't want a lawyer. The closest I can come to what he was working toward is a Barbie-doll wife."

Steve made a skeptical noise.

"I'm serious. For one thing, Barbie-wives don't have little sisters. Bo did everything he could to keep me out of Liz's life, starting with the 'no overnight guests' rule. Liz explained it to me the first time I invited myself for a visit. There were all sorts of crazy rules. For instance, he didn't allow her to wear sneakers, which was ridiculous. He discouraged her from forming friendships, and that was downright scary."

Steve looked unconvinced. "No sneakers? No friends?"

"Okay, I know it sounds like I'm the crazy one, but I'm serious. He disapproved, he discouraged, and he was not someone you wanted to make unhappy.

"There was one time I was allowed to visit. Liz was being honored for her 'Read to Your Kids' campaign. Bo didn't allow her to work, did you know that? So she volunteered. She started a statewide campaign to get parents to read to their children. Do you remember it? It got a lot of attention. There were ads on radio and TV, and she had the governor's wife and some celebrities involved. It was a big deal. I think Bo was of two minds about it; on the one hand, it indirectly brought him great press, and since he was planning his run for Congress, that was desirable, but the downside was that he had to share Liz." Pam spread her hands. "Barbie had flown the coop, and he saw his base—his home— threatened.

"When the state education association gave her an award, there was a big dinner—lots of important people. Liz insisted I come East for the affair, which was black tie, very posh. She was to give a short speech, so she was a little nervous but really up for it. We were at a table with all the big guns. Everyone was having a fine old time, and Bo started to relate a humorous incident that had happened to him and Liz earlier in the day. He was a great storyteller. His timing was usually flawless, but that night he kept hesitating, and at one point Liz stepped in and added a line or two. Bo turned to her, and there was this long pause. Then he said in a voice dripping ice, "You want to tell the story? Fine. Be my guest." Dead silence. No one knew where to look. Finally, the governor smoothed it over and conversation resumed. A couple minutes later the awards were announced, and Liz had to make her speech."

Steve whistled through his teeth. "Some timing."

"Exactly. And, of course, there were the kids. Bo thought consistency was the end-all in raising kids. Talk about rigidity, he was the poster boy. I think one of Liz's greatest accomplishments is how well adjusted Hugh and Harry are in spite of a father who was a control freak.

"When Bo's plane went down, Liz may have grieved, but she also knew that she was free." Pam leaned forward. "Can you imagine what that was like? Because you have to try in order to understand why she's so afraid to make a commitment to you.

"She no longer had Bo disparaging or arguing about everything in their lives. And I mean every. . .little. . . thing. One of Bo's favorite expressions was, 'Somebody's got to be in charge.' It must have been like being saved from death by smothering."

They contemplated their empty lunch dishes. After a time Steve said, "Why the hell didn't she divorce him?"

Pam made a sound of disgust. "Somewhere along the line, my sister got sucked into the religious aspect of her marriage vows—'til death do us part. I mean, Episcopal *priests* divorce, for God's sake, but not Liz."

Steve looked doubtful. "I don't know, Pam. Lizzie's self-confidence level is pretty high. Wouldn't living that way have destroyed any sense of self-worth she had?"

Pam nodded. "I've often wondered about that. She lived with his crap, and she never complained, never talked about him behind his back. Once I made some nasty comment about him in front of the kids, and she told me later to never do that, that the boys were as much Bo as they were her, and she didn't want them to hear him put down."

"But they must remember living with him. Hugh certainly would."

"Exactly my point to her. I said, 'Wouldn't it confuse them to paint a false picture of him?' and she said she never lied, but that there was no point in dwelling on the negative."

"Maybe there's some wisdom in that."

"Maybe."

"So Pam, what are you saying? Because you sure paint a grim picture."

"I have to tell you, I wouldn't be going to all this trouble if I didn't think you two were meant for each other." She gave him another radiant smile. "I know she's crazy about you. Have you seen her since the proposal fiasco?"

Steve shook his head.

"Talked to her?"

"No. I've been licking my wounds."

"What I'd do if I were you? I'd see her, be your sweet self, but stay away from the bedroom and all other sorts of intimacies. On the one hand, she'd know you cared, but on the other is the message that you might be thinking of moving on."

Steve looked doubtful. "That's it? You flew six hours to tell me I have to swear off sex?"

"No—to tell you not to give up. Liz will get the message that your relationship isn't going to go on as it was. Because that was to her liking—that, and nothing deeper."

Dr. Heller, four-oh-one, Dr. Steven Heller, four-oh-one.

"You have to go?"

"I do. Will you be around for a few days?"

She shook her head. "I'm flying back this evening. Keep in touch, and hang in there. I want to dance at the wedding."

He gave a humorless laugh. "God help me if I've got this all wrong and she starts seeing some CPA." Rising, he leaned down and kissed her. "Thanks, Pam. You're a good sister."

"You're welcome. Oh, and don't worry about the CPA. Didn't you know? Liz's middle name is Loyal."

27

BEAR MOUNTAIN

"HARRY, IF YOU FORGET TO BRING THAT PERMISSION SLIP home today, you will not—do you understand me?—you will not be allowed to go on this year's class trip tomorrow. No Bear Mountain Park." Lizzie squeezed a container of celery, carrots, and olives into Hugh's lunch bag, one of grapes and orange slices into Harry's, and turned her attention to bringing order to the cluttered counter. The usual confusion of a schoolday morning prevailed in the Donnely kitchen.

"Why do we have to have dumb old permission slips?" Harry smacked his cereal with the back of his spoon. "I think I lost mine."

Lizzie set his lunch box on the table and ruffled his hair. "That's just the way it is. If you want the pleasures of life, you have to do the groundwork. And your groundwork includes taking

responsibility for getting a permission slip home, signed, and back
to school. Explain the problem to Ms. Altman and ask her for a
new one."

That afternoon when she got home, she was relieved to find the
permission slip, worse for wear, but still legible, on the kitchen
table. She dumped her bags on a chair, signed it, and tucked it into
his backpack.

Checking the answering machine on her way upstairs, she
found two messages: one from Karen Altman, Harry's teacher, and
the other from Steven. She called Karen, who wanted to make sure
that the permission slip had gotten home. Lizzie assured her that
it had and thanked her for her patience. She'd wait to return
Steven's call until she had changed into something comfortable and
gotten dinner started.

Pulling on a tee shirt, she thought about him, about the uneasi-
ness that had developed between them since his proposal. The
proposal. . .it had been a bullet she'd known was coming but had
been unable to dodge. And it threatened to blow out of the water
the fine balance she'd finally achieved between freedom and love.
Her children were part of her and always had been, but now she
carried Steven tucked away in her heart, enriching her life as she'd
never thought possible. Yet the freedom, surprising her with the
joy it brought, was new and fragile and needed to be guarded.

As she slipped into jeans, she heard a commotion from below.

"Mom! Steve's here!" Hugh yelled up the staircase.

Halfway down the stairs, she could see that something was up.
"You look like the kid who's just won a trip to Disney World."

"Yep, I'm on my way—only it's Boston." His pleasure was evi-
dent. He leaned over the newel post and grinned up at her.

"You heard from Dr. Callaway." She sat down on the bottom step.

"This afternoon. He wants to see all our paperwork on Saturday. He still has one or two reservations about the reporting aspect, so Sam and I are spending tonight going over everything." He joined her on the step. "I won't be able to make dinner tomorrow night. We're going to fly up right after office hours. How about Sunday night? Who knows? We might be able to celebrate. Can you do that?"

She smiled, caught up by his obvious excitement. "Sure. Steven, I'm so happy for you. All that work. It's great news."

"It's not a done deal, but I have a real good feeling about it. Charles Callaway will demand that every 'i' is dotted, and I think Sam and I have done that."

Joining her on the porch as she waved good bye, Hugh asked, "What's Steve so hyper about?"

"He has a lot of work to do on his project."

"And he's happy because he gets to do a lot of work? Weird."

"Well, he's happy because it looks like he's going to get the approval he needs."

"Oh. Can I sleep over at Michael's tomorrow night? We want to watch the Yankee game."

"If it's all right with Michael's mother, and if you promise to keep noise to a respectable level, so you don't drive his folks crazy."

"Yeah, sure, okay. Thanks, Mom." He bounded down the porch steps and disappeared around the corner of the house.

Friday was one of those long days, the kind when anything that can go wrong did. She still managed to get home before four, pulling into the driveway with a quiet, solitary evening planned.

"Liz!" Angelica called from the top of the porch steps, her feet apart and her legs braced as though to withstand a strong wind. "Hurry!" She was clutching the cordless phone to her chest, and there was a shiver of panic in her voice.

"You must call this number. Is about Harry—something happened. The principal, he said, 'Have her call me at once. Is important.'" Angelica thrust the cordless receiver into her hand.

Lizzie grasped it, unable at first to punch in the numbers Angelica had written on a piece of scratch paper she was holding out to her.

"Liz? Bob Jacobs." She barely recognized the strained voice. "Liz, they called me from the park. Harry's gotten separated from the group. The park rangers are organizing a search, and—"

"*Separated?* What's that mean? He's *missing?* They've lost him? In the *woods?*" Her voice rose until it disappeared, and she clutched the phone, which was doing a jittery dance against her ear. She reached for the top step and sat down.

Hugh came up the walk. "What's wrong, Mom?"

She shook her head and tried to process what Bob was saying.

"...it's really best if you stay put. I'll call as soon as I hear anything. Liz? Did you hear what I said?"

"Yes—no! I'm sure it's a...a mistake. That's it. I bet they have him. Karen wouldn't lose him. I'm sure he's okay. He's probably on his way home right now." She heard herself jabbering and forced herself to stop. "Yes. All right. Call me. I'll be right here."

"Mom, Harry's lost? On Bear Mountain?"

"It's okay. It's going to be okay." She handed him the phone. She could feel her heart racing and knew she had to calm down.

"Here, Liz, drink this." Angelica wrapped her hands around a hot mug. "Is strong tea. Harry, he will be okay." She sat down on the step beside Lizzie and put an arm around her. "That Harry, such a little devil he is." She began to cry, her sobs shaking both of them.

Lizzie patted Angelica's back. "It's okay, I know it'll be okay," she said, assuring herself as well as Angelica.

"You should call Steve, Mom." Hugh tried to give her the phone.

"Steve?" She shook her head. "No. He's in Boston—he can't help."

"Well. . .what're we going to do?"

She saw how pale the boy was, could have counted every freckle on his face. Beside her, Angelica sniffled. She took a few deep breaths. "We'll wait for Mr. Jacobs to call and say Harry's on his way home to us. For Harry's sake, all three of us need to be calm. And ready. Just in case they want us to drive to Bear Mountain to get him." She was amazed at the firmness of her voice, when she could feel her insides breaking loose from their appointed places, roiling against each other.

He eyed her doubtfully. "Just wait? Can't we do something? Mickey's a hunter—maybe we could take him up there."

"We'll see," she said, tempted to smile. At that very moment, Mickey was chasing a large bug in the yard.

"*I* could call Steve."

"No, Hugh. I don't want you doing that. We can manage."

Hugh dug at the porch step with the toe of his sneaker. "Okay. I'm going to go to Michael's for a minute. I'll be right back. You'll call me?"

"Right away." She hugged him, suddenly very aware of the fragility of his bones, the spareness of his frame. "I'm glad you're here, Hugh."

She put in a call to Annie at church. Her own prayers consisted of two words, "Please, God," repeated so often that surely, she thought, a few of them got through. They were all she was capable of, while the hands of the clock moved as though mired in sludge, and her brain alternated between refusing to function or imagining Harry in unspeakable distress.

When Bob Jacobs called, it only deepened her despair. "No sign of him yet, I'm afraid," he reported, "but we're lucky with the light. It won't get dark for another couple hours."

Darkness. She hadn't considered it. Harry alone in the woods, that was bad enough, but in the dark? At some point she became aware of Hugh, sitting across from her at the kitchen table. He had changed into hiking boots and a heavy sweatshirt.

"Hugh, I think we'd better drive up there. But first you should eat something."

"I don't want anything, Mom. I think I want to stay here. You should stay, too. You shouldn't drive there. And what if we'd get there, and Harry'd be on his way home, and we wouldn't be here. *Please*, Mom?"

She tried to figure it out. If only her head were working. "All right, let's wait a little longer. It's just that if it gets dark. . . ." She couldn't finish.

At some point in the early evening Angelica fixed them sandwiches and heated a pot of soup. Annie called and insisted on joining them. Jen, too, wanted to sit with her, but Lizzie flagged her off. "Please, just say prayers for Harry, lots of them. I'll call as soon as I hear anything."

By the time Annie got there, Lizzie could barely move. All of her senses had retreated, curling inward for safety, and, although she sat at the kitchen table with the three of them—Angelica, Annie, and Hugh—she couldn't eat, couldn't process what they were saying, and playing in her head were scenes of Harry floundering in the darkness. She barely noticed Steve coming in, Biz and Mickey trailing him with welcoming tails.

When he knelt beside her chair, she turned to him, slowly focusing her eyes.

"Oh, Steven, Harry's lost."

He took both of her hands and held them tightly. "I stopped to see how you were holding up. I'm going to check on things at the park. I'd like to take Hugh along. Will you be okay? You have Angelica and Annie with you."

"If only Bob Jacobs would call. They must have found him by now."

"Lizzie, Harry knows. . .he understands about not going with strangers?"

She couldn't speak, the implication was so awful. Finally she nodded her head.

"Does he know the park? Have you been there with him?"

"No. He's been to Tallman, but not Bear Mountain."

He stood up, holding onto her hands. "Come, walk to the car with me." Turning to Annie, he put a piece of paper on the table. "Those are my cell phone and pager numbers. I'll try and keep you posted, but don't hesitate to call me. . .for any reason."

With an arm around Lizzie, he walked her out to the driveway. She saw that Hugh was sitting in the passenger seat of the car, a backpack on his lap, the seat belt secured.

Steve held her close for a moment. "You can do this, Lizzie, I know you can. You're the strongest person I know. I'll call the minute we get there." He held her face between his hands and kissed her.

She watched his headlights sweep down the driveway and then across the lawn as he turned into the street. Nearly dark already, it would be completely so by the time they reached Bear Mountain.

A short time later Lizzie's phone took on a life of its own, ringing nearly nonstop. She didn't argue when Annie insisted on answering. They were mostly calls from parents of friends and classmates of Harry and Hugh. Soon, however, reporters began to call. To them Harry was not only a six-year-old lost boy, but the son of a past state senator who had died tragically on the eve of breaking into national politics. And since there had recently been two widely reported abductions of children, Harry's disappearance was newsworthy. By midnight the hot white lights of a television mobile unit lit the front of the house to daylight brilliance and added to Lizzie's sensation of having wakened to a nightmare.

28

CLIMBING

"HEY, STEVE?"

"Uh-huh?"

"I'm sorry about your meetings and all."

Steve glanced sideways at his passenger, and a wave of tenderness engulfed him. Hugh had slicked back his hair, probably with
gel; was wearing his faded NFL sweat shirt, which Steve knew was
his favorite; and was clutching a Boy Scout flashlight in one hand,
a Swiss army knife in the other.

"That's okay, Hugh. Dr. Kaufman will handle our end just fine.
You did the right thing. Harry's a lot more important than those
meetings. You and your mom, too."

"She said not to call."

"Yeah, well, once in awhile parents are wrong. Rarely, understand, but once in awhile." He smiled at the boy.

Hugh grinned.

"I'm impressed by how you tracked me down. Usually the women who run our office aren't very forthcoming about doctors' whereabouts."

"I told them I was Mrs. Donnely's son, and that it was a big emergency and I lost your pager number."

"You did good, Hugh."

"Will we go into the woods tonight, do you think? 'Cause Harry'll be pretty scared. All alone out there." His voice caught, and he turned and looked out the side window.

"We'll have to see when we get there." Steve didn't want to think of Harry alone and scared, as Hugh said, or worse—in the wrong hands. The images drained him, and he knew the space would quickly fill with fear, a luxury he couldn't afford.

When they arrived at the main building, a sprawling lodge, the woman at the main desk directed them to what she called the 'command post' and to Ed Reyes, the ranger in charge of the search. The center, on the ground floor and reached through an entrance from the back parking lot, was damp and had a low ceiling, tile floor, and small windows high up on the outer wall. Illuminated only by individual lamps on the desks and tables, Steve felt as though he'd entered a cave. A man who looked to be in charge sat at a desk near the entrance, holding a phone to his ear with a shoulder while typing on the keyboard of a laptop. He introduced himself as Reyes and motioned Steve and Hugh to chairs at the side of the desk. Dressed in the heavy brown twill shirt of a ranger, he was a tall man and gaunt, his face as if in mourning, with deep-set, hooded eyes that revealed nothing. Steve had spoken with him earlier, on the phone, from Logan Airport.

Reyes replaced the phone, rose, and extended his hand. After explaining what was being done to find Harry, he said, "A few of the fellows are going to make one more trip out tonight. They'll stick to main trails. You and the boy are welcome to go along." He flicked a glance at Steve's clothes, a suit and tie meant for a hospital conference room. "You'll be needing boots. A warm jacket, too. Gets cold out in the woods. See if you can find something to fit you in there." He pointed with his chin to a door behind them.

The door led to a small room notable for its Spartan neatness. A variety of coats and jackets hung from hooks along one wall, and lined up on the floor beneath the coats were pairs of boots in varying sizes and states of wear. Steve found jackets for himself and Hugh and settled on a pair of boots, that though stiff and worn, seemed to fit. He dialed Lizzie's number before returning to Reyes. Annie answered.

"How's she doing?"

"I'm getting us all a little drunk on wine, and that's helping. What's going on up there?"

He told her that the search was going to continue until midnight and repeated the news to Lizzie when she got on the line. She sounded less stricken than when he talked with her at the house; perhaps the wine was helping.

The night turned into a kaleidoscope of movement with no connection to the world as he knew it. Outside on the parking lot rangers and volunteers milled around in what seemed a disorganized manner, but everyone ended up in the right place. Steve and Hugh joined a team of four and set out on a wide trail that narrowed after several hundred yards. As the lights from the lodge faded, the beams of their flashlights took over with not much help from a moon that rode behind a thin curtain of clouds. Except for periodic stops when their repeated shouts of Harry's name exploded into the darkness of trees and brush, they were a silent group, accompanied only by the sound of boots tamping down the trails' damp soil and the occasional crack of a broken branch.

By midnight they had made a wide circle, ending up back at the lodge, where the trucks and camera lights of the media, its members hunkered down for the duration, were fanned out along the periphery of the parking lot.

Some of the searchers were using cots in the infirmary to catch a few hours' sleep. Steve settled Hugh there, then returned to the main room. He talked with Reyes about past searches in the park, spoke to one of the EMS team that had been called in, drank too much bitter coffee, and, finally, took a cot next to Hugh's, hoping to get a couple hours sleep before daybreak, when the search would be renewed. The problem was his brain, which had taken on a life of its own, racing along as though dosed on amphetamines. He was familiar with the sensation, had had it often enough in periods of stress. He longed for an off switch, knowing he needed rest but unable to get it.

He had finally managed a light, troubled sleep when he heard his name and struggled to consciousness to find Reyes leaning over him in a room filled with the pearly gray of early morning.

"We're ready to roll—you said to give you a call. Better leave your boy sleep. May be rough going."

Steve pushed himself up on one elbow and squinted at his watch. Rolling off the cot, he checked that Hugh was okay and pulled the rough wool blanket up over the boy's shoulder. It was cold. He wondered how Harry had made it through the night.

This time they didn't stick to the main trails. As Steve worked to keep up, he thought that Reyes should probably have wakened Hugh, who he was certain could do a better job getting through the woods than he was doing. When they returned to the lodge in mid-morning, he found Hugh sitting on a stone wall outside the entrance.

"Should of woke me," the boy said, moving over and making room for him. He looked straight ahead, avoiding Steve's eyes, his expression conveying hurt as well as anger.

Steve nodded. "You're right. I'm sorry." They were quiet for a spell, one weary of doing nothing and the other just plain weary. "Did you get something to eat?" Steve asked, breaking the silence.

"Yeah. They have lots of food."

"I'm going to wash up and get some coffee. Then we'll call your mom."

It wasn't a conversation he was happy about having. Lizzie sounded like glass ready to shatter, and what good was he? He felt useless and a fool into the bargain. He'd raced to the scene as if he alone could put matters right—rescue Harry, deliver him to Lizzie, and what? Be the hero? As it was, he had nothing to tell her, no words to strengthen her resolve or bring her comfort. So he assured her that Hugh was fine, and that not only were rangers combing the woods, but also volunteers, who were arriving by the busload. He urged her—gently, for she sounded so fragile—to get some sleep.

He and Hugh joined the volunteers and spent the afternoon tramping the woods. Though it was cloudy, the heat and insects made the going rough. Dogs, brought in to pick up Harry's scent, coursed the trails, and overhead a helicopter endlessly circled. By the end of the afternoon Steve was as weary as Hugh. The noise, fresh air, physical activity, and stress overpowered his intention to continue, and after a cold supper, they sought out cots in the infirmary and slept.

He woke at dusk to the sound of rain pelting the windows. Any prospect of further sleep was washed away along with some of his hope for a good outcome. In the main room the atmosphere was cheerless, the rangers wet and dispirited. Missing were the energy and optimism of the night before. Ed Reyes was hunched over his desk, a phone to his ear. Steve got himself a cup of coffee, found a quiet corner, and dialed Lizzie's number. Her friend Jen answered and told him that Lizzie had finally fallen asleep.

"Stay with her, will you, Jen? She shouldn't be alone."

He wasn't able to keep his thoughts from Harry, and the couple hours of sleep he had grabbed had been fitful and had done nothing to replenish his strength. When the rain tapered off to an annoying drizzle, preparations were made for another search. He splashed water on his face, drank coffee for its restorative powers—certainly not for its flavor—and was about to force a foot into one of the stiff boots when he heard loud voices coming from outside. Reyes beckoned to him with a wave of the arm.

"We have him! He's alive."

29

HOSPITAL

A FEW HARDY RANGERS, ignoring the rain, had found Harry several hundred feet up a steep incline about two miles from the lodge. Steve struggled up the nearly vertical slope, using wet shrubs and clumps of slippery grass as his handrail and digging into the wet dirt with his boots. Harry was in a small space under an overhang that had been created by a rocky ledge. The needles of a stunted fir made a soft bed for him, and he lay clutching a Boy Scout thermos in his muddy hands.

There was barely enough space under the ledge for the rangers, one seated on the ground beside the boy, who she'd wrapped in her jacket and two others, who had dug out footholds and were using the ledge for support.

Steve sank to his knees and took the woman's place. Under

lights held by the rangers, Harry peered at him, one eye swollen shut and the other badly bloodshot. An egg-sized lump stood out on his forehead. His cheeks were a battleground of scratches and tear tracks, and his lower lip was split and oozing blood.

"Steve," he whispered.

"It's okay, Harry. You're going to be okay." Steve's hands were already checking him. "Did you knock yourself out, Harry?"

"My leg—"

Steve had to bend closer to hear him.

"My leg. . .hurts."

"You couldn't walk on it, right?"

"They didn't hear me. . .my backpack. . . ." He pointed toward the base of the hill.

Steve moved aside and let the EMS people take over.

One of the rangers said, "The backpack is how we found him. It was in some tall grass that the rain had flattened. We'd been by here before but we didn't see it."

"If it hadn't rained. . . ." Steve didn't finish.

"Yeah," the ranger said. "Kid must have fallen off this ledge, then dragged himself under it."

One of the EMS team rose and told Steve, "His vitals are good, considering what he's been through. But he must have hit his head pretty hard to get a swelling like that."

"Okay, hold off on water. Start an IV and let's splint the leg and see if we can get him off this mountain and back to the lodge."

Hugh had just wakened when Steve returned to the infirmary.

"Come see your brother, Hugh. He's asking for you."

A Medi-Vac helicopter sat on the parking lot, rotors turning.

"Holy shit, Harry! Your face is totally awesome!" Hugh declared.

Steve yelled over the noise, "Hugh, you can ride with Harry if you'd like. They're taking him to a hospital in the city, and your mom will be there. What do you say?"

"Are you going, too?"

"No, there's not a lot of room. I'm going to drive. You can come with me, if you'd rather."

Hugh's eyes traveled between Steve and the helicopter. "You don't care if I go with Harry?"

"I think Harry would like to have you with him."

"Yeah, me too."

Steve put an arm around him and hugged him. A look of pleasure fought one of embarrassment on Hugh's sleep-creased face. "Get going, Hugh, or you'll miss your ride."

"Yeah—bye, Steve. And thanks."

Steve watched him race across the lot, his hair whipped back from the force of the air that the rotors were making out of a quiet mountain breeze.

The drive into the city seemed interminable. Lizzie could barely speak to Annie, who had insisted on getting her to the hospital.

"He's going to be okay." Annie reached across the gearshift and patted her clenched hands. "Steve said it was probably a mild concussion. He said Harry was conscious, didn't he?"

"Yes. He talked to him, but still. . .his head. . . ."

Once at the hospital, she was directed to the floor Harry would be taken to. She found an empty waiting room and sat on the edge of one of the chairs. A television set was tuned to one of the cable news shows. Someone had muted the volume, leaving the secretary of state and a panel of journalists engaged in a soundless exchange. City lights worked their way through the New York grime on the windows at the far end of the room. Leaning back in the chair, she forced herself to take deep breaths, but still couldn't seem to get enough air into her lungs. And although she closed her eyes, the smells and sounds scaled her defenses and took her back to that January with Katie in Port Smith Hospital.

The minutes crept by. A nurse came over to her and pointed out a room across the hall, where, she told Lizzie, there was hot water for tea or coffee. "Why not get yourself a cup? It may be awhile." Lizzie managed a smile. It was too much of an effort to speak, and the thought of swallowing anything made her stomach do uncomfortable turns.

Time crept by, until finally a young man in scrubs appeared. "Mrs. Donnely? Your little boy's here now. Want to come with me?" She followed him around several bends in the hall until she saw Hugh standing with a nurse beside a gurney.

Lizzie didn't gasp or wince when she saw Harry's face. "I was so happy to see you," she told him later, "it wouldn't have mattered if you'd grown five eyes and three noses." She wanted to pick him up and feel the weight of him in her arms against her body; wanted to carry him away, whole again and safe. Instead she ran her hands through his muddy hair and kissed him gently. Holding his hands to her cheeks, she whispered his name, trying to get control of her voice.

"Mom, I fell."

"Oh, sweetheart, I know."

"Am I being brave?"

"Yes, you're being *very* brave." She felt the band, which had tightened around her chest when Angelica called to her from the porch, begin to loosen.

"Do I have to stay here? I wanna go home."

She leaned over him and stroked his cheek. "For a little while, Harry, just a little while."

"It hurts, Mom." Tears began to roll down the sides of his face into his hair.

Lizzie fought back her own tears.

"We'll need to take him now," the nurse said.

"Hugh and I will be here, Harry. We'll see you real soon."

Again the waiting, but it was easier, now that she had seen him. At some point Steven came to take them to him. As they hurried along, he explained the results of the tests to her.

His first words were, "A mild concussion, no serious brain injury," and for a moment the floor tilted and sound swirled in her head.

They found Harry bathed and in a hospital gown, an IV bag swinging from a gleaming bar overhead. His open eye was nearly all black pupil, wide and frightened. He grasped her hand.

"Harry, remember when you fell, how your leg hurt?"

"I couldn't even walk on it, so I stayed right there under that little cliff."

"That's right. Well, one of your leg bones broke, and it's not lined up the way it should be. The doctors are going to give you something to make you sleep, and they'll operate on it. They know exactly how to fix it. They said they have a pair of silver crutches you can have, when it's time to walk again."

She watched him as he thought about the crutches.

"All my own?"

"Yes, you can keep them."

His lower lip, swollen and still seeping a watery blood, began to tremble. "You come, too, Mom."

"Oh, Harry, I'm not allowed." She looked over at Steve, and he nodded. "Steven's here. He'll stay with you."

"I'll be right beside you, Harry."

"When they operate?"

"Every minute."

"Can you hold my hand, Steve?"

He nodded. "Sure. Sure I can."

Lizzie put his hand in Steve's, bent and kissed his bruised forehead, then stepped back as the attendant pushed the gurney through swinging doors.

30

KITCHEN

HARRY CAME HOME FROM THE HOSPITAL in the sunshine and warmth of a Sunday in mid-June, a day when the homes on Stelfox Street appeared to have emptied their inhabitants onto the sidewalks and lawns. Children tore about, euphoric in their deliverance from school; grown-ups worked on lawns and visited over fences. Word of Harry's imminent arrival spread quickly.

Emily Craig remembered that she had a Mickey Mouse cake in her freezer, one she had bought when she thought her grandson was coming to visit. "Just the thing," she told her husband. "Liz has been so busy, she probably didn't have time to pick up a cake." Nancy Gould handed Angelica a box of party favors left over from her son Chucky's birthday celebration. Hugh and Michael coasted up the driveway with helium-filled balloons attached to the handlebars of their bicycles. With the help of the neighborhood children, they tied balloons to trees, bushes, and the railings of the Donnelys' front porch.

Harry didn't disappoint the crowd. He emerged from the car on shining aluminum crutches that reflected sharp glitters of sunlight. Streamers of bright ribbons, which the pediatric nurses had tied to them, fluttered in the breeze. Harry's head was a confusion of dreadlocks, the work of the nurses' aides, who had been enchanted by his abundant silver hair. And emblazoned on the chest of his blue and orange shirt, a stylishly too large gift from Aunt Pam, was the Mets logo. Had the sun not been shining, Harry's wide and delighted smile would have handled the job.

Liz and Jen stood in the driveway and let Hugh and Michael escort him to the porch, where, to the cheers of his admiring audience, he navigated the steps.

Jen grinned. "A lot like Caesar entering Rome after crossing the Rubicon, don't you think?"

"Exactly," Liz agreed.

Steve finished Thursday evening office hours by ten but stayed on at his desk, catching up on paperwork. Since Port Smith had received the go-ahead as one of the Mass General study sites, he hadn't had time for much else. Which was good, because it had been nearly two weeks since Harry came home, and although Steve called Lizzie often, he'd only succeeded in reaching the answering machine—and his messages went unanswered. The two times he'd gone to the house, Angelica had met him at the door to explain that Lizzie was resting. "Is not to be disturbed," she'd said apologetically, her wide dark eyes saddened by the message. Furious one minute, worried sick the next, he felt emotionally drained by the events of the last month.

It was nearly midnight when he got to Aspenhill. Too late to see her, yet he turned onto Stelfox. The soft lemon-colored glow of the streetlights shone through fully leafed trees, and most of the houses, including Lizzie's, sat in darkness. But when he pulled into the driveway intending to turn around, he noticed a splatter of light from the kitchen on the back lawn. Without pausing to consider the wisdom of his move, he shut off the motor. Swaying shadows of leaves and bushes moved silently on the floorboards of the porch. He found the inner door open, the screen unlatched, and reasoned that if he called her name, the dogs would erupt, waking the boys. He stepped in. A night-light cast a faint glow on the stairs to the second floor. Music—a tenor sax softly singing the blues—drifted from the back of the house. Hesitating only briefly, he found his way down the darkened hall to the kitchen.

The windows over the sink were open to the night air, which stirred the curtains and filled the room with the fragrance of fading roses. Lizzie sat at the table in a circle of light, papers and notebooks spread in front of her, a pen in her right hand. The hand was still, her thoughts appeared to be elsewhere. He stood and gazed at her—reading glasses slipping down her nose, hair a riot of curls in the humidity of early summer, face pale and serious. The realization of how much he had missed her perversely fueled his anger.

"Lizzie," he said quietly and watched her eyes widen with surprise and heard the quick intake of her breath.

"Sorry, didn't mean to frighten you. But you aren't answering your phone. And you don't return my calls. I guess I'm to understand there's a message in there somewhere." He was conscious of his breathing, how the exhalations shook him. "Is that right?" She stared at him, not responding. He couldn't read her expression. "Lizzie?"

She continued to look at him, and he thought she wasn't going to speak. But then without taking her eyes from his, she set the pen down and said, "You're right."

The refrigerator began to hum. In the distance a dog barked. Weariness, like a familiar blanket, wrapped itself around him. "What's wrong, Lizzie?"

She shook her head.

"Don't do that. What's *wrong?*"

"You won't understand. I know I don't, so how can I explain?"

"Try."

She began straightening the papers and books in front of her. "I think. . .I'm on overload. Harry lost. . .the end of school. . .these reports. . . ." She gestured at the stack of papers. "And hanging over all of it. . . ." She looked up at him. "Hanging over all of it is your proposal." Gripping the edge of the table, she said, "I need time, Steven. But you're right. I haven't been kind or fair, and it's. . . ." She shook her head again, unable to continue.

Now he could see the tears. He looked at her eyes, a remarkable blue, the irises rimmed in black. He felt such grief at that moment, such loss. He asked himself if he could turn away and never see those eyes again. Yet he couldn't keep on hitting his head against a stone wall. He'd reached the end of trying.

She relaxed her grip on the table. "I saw Sam yesterday." At his sharp look, she said, "No, it's nothing, just dizziness, an allergy." She waved it away. "He told me Hugh called you in Boston. . .about Harry. I didn't know. I guess I was too upset that night to question why you were suddenly there. Hugh shouldn't have called you. That meeting with Dr. Callaway was too important to you."

He looked at her for a long moment, feeling anger spread through him, tasting it as it reached his mouth. "If you think for one minute that the fucking meeting was more important than Harry—" He stopped and put a hand over his eyes for a moment before continuing, the sharpness drained from his voice. "*You* should have called me."

"No." She leaned forward, her voice low but intense. "I appreciate your help, but you have to understand—I can manage. I can take care of my family. . .and I can take care of myself."

"Great! You manage. And don't worry how that affects everyone around you."

"What does that mean? What are you talking about?"

"I'm talking about Hugh and Harry. . .and Will. I'm talking about me. Maybe the kids would like to have something more. . .a dad. . .a mother. Maybe they'd like to be a whole family."

She said nothing. The silence grew. She studied him with narrowed eyes. Finally she asked, "And you, Steven. . .what do you want?"

The clock in the hall chimed. He waited until it had stopped. "I want to live with you. I want more than a drop-by-on-Friday-night kind of relationship." His voice broke. "I love you. It's that simple."

Footsteps pattered overhead, followed by the noise of a toilet flushing. Lizzie pushed back her chair. Rising, she looked at him closely. "Sit down. I'll get you a cup of tea—or would you like something stronger?"

He shook his head. "No, tea would be good. Thanks." He

reached for a chair.

She put a flame under the kettle. "Harry isn't your responsibility. The Donnelys aren't your worry. You have Will to care for, your profession to consider. I know how important getting that study is to you."

"We got it, you know."

"Sam told me."

They were quiet waiting for the water to boil. After she prepared the tea, she joined him at the table.

"You want too much from me, Steven," she said quietly. "You want more than I'm capable of giving. You *deserve* more than I can give."

"That's simply not true."

"I think it is."

He watched the translucent wings of a small moth beat against the light shade.

"I know there are thousands and thousands of women in worse situations than I was in. I know that. But for me, living with Bo became. . .it was like water torture. I never knew when the next drop would fall, only that it would. He sucked up my space. I didn't dream, I couldn't enjoy my life. I spent the dreaming time preparing what I needed to say to Bo to explain why things hadn't gone as he expected them to go, because they never did. . .they never did." Her voice had faded to a whisper.

"He's gone. That's all over, it's *over*, Lizzie."

She stared at him for a moment, then dropped her eyes. "My brain knows it's over, but not my insides. . .my heart. . .whatever. I know it was Bo who. . . ." She waved a hand. "Somewhere deep inside, I feel I was the problem." She raised her eyes and looked directly at him. "That's the part of me that doesn't want to be married. Don't you see? I'm afraid to gamble my dreams."

Steve could hear one of the dogs snuffling in his sleep in the den, could hear the clock in the hall ticking, the occasional car going by, but he couldn't hear what he should be thinking, what he should say.

Her voice barely audible, she said, "The trouble is you're the best friend I have. The trouble is. . .I love you."

"Lizzie."

"Can't we just go on? Can't we just be good friends?" She stopped as he raised a skeptical eyebrow. "Okay, *very* good friends." And she had the grace to smile.

"Tell me. . .can you tell me why that won't work?"

She gazed at him for a long moment. "I know. The boys."

He nodded. "You know, Lizzie, that day Harry got lost—it wasn't like hearing that a friend's son was lost. It was like losing a son. I could never have sat through meetings and dinner knowing that Harry was alone or in grave danger. I had to get to him. That's why I want all of you, each and every Donnely." He smiled. "Even those two sorry excuses for watchdogs."

She took a deep, shuddering breath. ". . . I was so frightened."

"I know."

"When Katie got sick, and I rushed her to the hospital—all through those terrible hours I believed nothing bad would come of it. Can you imagine? I knew she was very, very sick, but. . .die? No. I wasn't able to believe that was a possibility." She paused, and he could see that she was breathing rapidly. "I kept thinking of that as I waited to hear. . .you know, about Harry." She dropped her head into her hands.

Steve strained to hear her.

"I thought. . .if I keep believing he's going to be okay, will it be like Katie. . . ?"

He lifted her head, wiped her tears with his handkerchief, then handed it to her.

"You're not going to have any of these left," she said through her tears. "I have quite a collection."

"How can I make you understand? Nothing—no one is more important to me than you and our boys, all three of them." He reached a hand across the space between them. "I told you I'd never fail you. I meant it, Lizzie."

She looked down at his hand on the table. "What are we going to do?"

"I don't know. Give it some time? Return my calls?"

She covered his hand with both of hers.

31

SPRING LAKE

"WHAT DO YOU THINK? A FRIENDLY COTTAGE?" Steve turned to Lizzie, who was leaning forward against the Audi's seat belt, peering through the windshield at the weathered Cape Cod that sat outlined against a fading sun.

Eyes narrowed in concentration, she took her time, studying each window, the chimney, the rose shrubs that crowded the path to the front door. "Umm, yes, I think so—friendly but forlorn."

He raised an eyebrow and one corner of his mouth. "Okay, why forlorn?"

"Well, for one thing, all those dead roses. No one's bothered to prune them. And for another, the window shades are pulled to different lengths, as though a neat appearance isn't worth the extra effort." She turned to him. "Can't you see that?"

He didn't reply and instead looped an arm around her shoulders and pulled her close.

She took a deep breath of the sea air. "I keep expecting to hear your pager beeping—or Harry asking another of his questions."

"And you thought you'd feel too guilty to enjoy yourself."

"I was wrong." She had hesitated when he suggested they go away for a night toward the end of July. It'd been a difficult month and had seemed endless. Harry had needed physical therapy at the hospital in the city, and that had wiped out their annual vacation in Nantucket. As though to rub in the loss, the weather had been ferocious—humid ninety-degree days with little relief at night.

"I'm sure Angelica can manage for twenty-four hours without you," he had argued.

"Where did you have in mind?"

"Not far. There's a cottage in Spring Lake we can use."

"I don't know—Harry on crutches, that's a lot for Angelica to manage. I wouldn't enjoy myself."

"Don't worry about it. I'll be in charge of enjoyment. You can see the ocean from the terrace of this place. Both of us need some R and R."

"Don't forget my bag," she called to him as they got out of the car.

"We'll get it later. You probably won't need it. We're only here one night."

"Not *need* it? All my stuff is in it—my nightgown, my make-up. . .what?" His amused expression had stopped her.

"Nightgown? You seriously brought a nightgown?"

"Yes, I brought a nightgown. I don't sleep in the nude," she said defensively, feeling foolish as soon as the words were out.

"No exceptions? Okay, okay," he said hastily, opening the trunk. "I'll get your bag. With the nightgown in it."

They took a brick path around the side of the house to a terrace paved with flagstones and edged with terra cotta pots overflowing with crimson ivy geraniums, which trailed gracefully onto the lawn. There was wrought iron furniture set out, and the glass top of a table was reflecting the crimson streaks of the setting sun.

Steve unlocked the French doors, and they entered, finding themselves in a large open room. A couch, two comfortable looking chairs and a coffee table filled the front end of the room, with a large, round, pine table and assorted straight-back chairs occupying the end closest to the terrace. On the tables glass pitchers overflowed with summer flowers and filled the air with their sweet scents.

After putting Lizzie's bag in the bedroom, Steve went into the kitchen, and, humming contentedly, began to open doors and drawers, clinking utensils, china, and glass.

Lizzie leaned against the counter and watched him put their dinner together. He placed bowls of gazpacho on a tray along with small glass dishes of chopped onion, green pepper, and parsley.

They ate outdoors, savoring the soup in the flickering light of candles, which Steve had lit and set in hurricane glasses to protect the flames from the steady breeze. When they finished, he took the bowls back to the kitchen. "I'm going to stir fry some scallops while you get the salads from the refrigerator."

She found three covered bowls of various vegetable salads and took them out to the table. When she returned, she was met by the aroma of basil and garlic. "Where did all this food come from? No, I'm not going to question it, or it may disappear."

"And we'd have to order from Dominoes—yeah, good point." He cut thick slices of French bread, buttered them and put them on a pan in the toaster oven.

Later, while coffee dripped, he slipped several CDs into the player.

"Is that Fred Astaire?" she asked.

"That's him. I like his voice." He settled a sweater around her shoulders. "Getting chilly."

Fred sang while they drank their coffee.

"Lizzie, I have a confession you need to hear. I lied to you, and it's the only time I've done that. Other than one time when you asked me if I liked something you were wearing, and I said 'yes,' but. . .I'm sorry. . .it was awful."

She was quiet for a moment, fond exasperation toying with the corners of her mouth. "All right, tell me about the big lie."

"This goes back to our first dinner together—we were in the car. You said you were afraid you wouldn't be able to meet my expectations."

Her eyes narrowed in thought. "And you said. . .you had no expectations. But you did? Is that it?"

"I did."

They gazed at one another for a long moment, then he reached across the table and took her hand. "Dance with me."

She slipped into his arms. "What's Fred singing?"

"It's called 'From This Moment On.' Listen." *From this moment on, you for me, dear. . . .From this happy day, no more blue songs. . . .For you've got the love I need so much. . . .*

She leaned back a little so that she could see his face. The candles and the moonlight were tracing shadows over it, and she realized how familiar it was to her now, how she knew each curve and hollow. *Got the arms to hold me tight. . . . Got the sweet lips to kiss me good night. . . . Every care is gone, from this moment on.*

Fred's voice faded into the night.

Long past midnight they lay in bed and watched through the open windows a quarter moon flirt with drifting clouds. "So many stars," Lizzie sighed. "We don't see that many in Aspenhill."

"All that reflected light from the city. Makes it hard to see them."

"Sad, isn't it?"

"Umm. Lizzie, are you okay with our sex life? It satisfies you? You enjoy it?"

She raised herself up on one elbow and stared down at him. "Yes—and yes and yes. Why do you need to ask? You don't. . . ?" She stopped but continued to look at him.

"Of course, yes, I love our sex life." He moved her elbow so that she lay back down. "I just want to cover all my bases, you know, in light of a possible future marriage. A change of heart?"

"Oh, Steven," she groaned. "This has been such a wonderful night. Please don't."

"I have to—but, okay, not tonight." He pulled the sheet over her shoulders. "Maybe in the morning?"

32

BASEMENT

THE DOOR TO THE STORAGE ROOM in the Donnelys' basement, rarely used and badly warped by time and damp, resisted Lizzie's initial efforts to open it. Finally, she rocked the stubborn wood up and down until it swung in. Darkness met her, and a dank, musty odor that settled in her nasal passages, reminding her why she disliked and avoided that corner of the house. But she had committed herself to cleaning it and wanted to do so before summer was suddenly autumn and she was back to school.

Cobwebs whispered across her face and hands as she fumbled for the light switch. In the instant before the bare light bulb went on, she heard a scrabbling sound in a far corner, setting off a shudder that started in her shoulders, rolled to her thighs, and caused her to lift her feet quickly, one after the other, in a dance of disgust.

I need a cat, she thought.

Even in low wattage the mess and confusion of the room were daunting. The temptation to back out nibbled at the edges of her resolve. She climbed onto one of the sturdier boxes and replaced the bulb with the brighter one she'd brought. It was a start. From that vantage she looked around, a reluctant general facing the enemy. Metal shelves stood against the walls, piled high with dis-carded toys, rusty garden tools, baby equipment she no longer needed, appliances that had been replaced by newer and shinier versions—the variety of items seemed endless. Cardboard boxes of varying shapes and sizes were set among pieces of broken or no longer used furniture. The bed she had shared with Bo lay there in pieces.

Harry found her before dinner. "Angelica says to tell you we can eat in fifteen minutes and do you want fresh broc'li or should she warm up the green beans? Hey! There's my Yogi Bear I've been looking for." He dropped his crutches and began to dig into the large box of items Lizzie intended for the next morning's trash pickup.

"I think broccoli, and you don't want that old thing, Harry. That's why it's down here." She pushed hair off her forehead with the back of her wrist. "Come on—leave that box alone and go tell Angelica about the broccoli."

"Okay, but I'm gonna come back and help."

She was sorting through a crate of Bo's law books when he returned. Within minutes he had half the contents of the trash box on the floor.

"Okay, Harry, here's the deal. You can sit and watch me work, or you can go back upstairs and help Angelica. What you *can't* do is go through that stuff, because I already have."

"Okay, okay, I'll watch." He flopped down on the old couch that was missing one of its feet, giving it a jaunty starboard list. "I told Steve I was going to be like him when I grow up."

She looked at him. He was bent over, examining the cartoons Hugh had drawn on his cast. From overhead she could hear Mickey chasing about.

"A doctor is a good thing to be."

"Yeah, but I mean a dad. If my little boy breaks his leg, I'm gonna hold his hand while the doctors operate on him." He laughed. "Look, Mom, here's where Hugh drew *me*."

"Yes, I see that. There you are on crutches." She held out a hand. "Let's go up and eat."

She returned to the basement after dinner. Steve had called to say that he was with a patient in the ICU and probably wouldn't make the movie they'd planned on seeing. By late evening she had managed to create some order in the room. She took a break, retreating to the couch, where she stretched out and thought about the hot shower she was going to stand under for several hours. She was sure there was dust in every pore of her body. The sound of movement overhead had died away, telling her that Angelica had managed to get the boys settled for the night. She considered the decision she'd made just a few hours earlier, and knew it was right. How simple, after all these month, she thought, and ironically, how liberating. Humming "Bye, Bye, Blackbird," she got up, found the broom, and began to sweep the floor.

"Underground jazz—I like it." He was standing in the doorway, collar unbuttoned and tie undone. "Thought I'd stop in and apologize for standing you up." He stepped around the mound of plastic bags and cartons that she'd filled. "Thinking of moving?"

"No, just some late spring cleaning." She put down the broom. "I'd better not kiss you—I'm a mess."

"It's okay. I have a thing for smudged cheeks."

She leaned forward, allowing only her lips to touch him, and felt the stubble of his beard against her mouth as she pulled away. "Did you eat?"

"Nope. Thought maybe you'd have some leftovers I could talk you out of."

"Lots of cold broccoli, but let's go up and look."

"It's okay. I'll get something at home."

"No, don't do that." She turned off the light and followed him out of the room. "Angelica poached salmon."

After she had set a plate of salmon, roasted potatoes, broccoli, and salad in front of him, she turned off the overhead lights, poured herself a cup of coffee and sat across from him. Rosemary, perfuming the air, drove away the musty basement odor. She watched him eat, relaxing in the silence.

"Coffee?" she asked, when he'd finished.

"Please. You don't know how good that tasted. It's been a long day and then the ICU on top of it—tiring and depressing."

"Probably worse than cleaning a basement." She handed him a mug of coffee.

"A draw, maybe. Let's go back to Spring Lake this weekend."

Lizzie raised an eyebrow, the corners of her mouth playing with a smile. "The romantic hideaway?"

He nodded. "Oh, yeah, and yes, I'm going to ask you to marry me. I figure it'll be a monthly thing—sooner or later you'll say 'yes' just to shut me up."

"Will you?"

"Yes, I'm not kidding."

"No—will you? Will you marry me, Steven?" She reached across the table and touched his cheek. "I know it's sudden. Take a few days. . .think about it."

33

PHILADELPHIA

"I HAVE TO SEE SOME PEOPLE AT UNIVERSITY HOSPITAL in Philadelphia next Saturday," Steve said as he stacked clean plates from the dishwasher. "Won't Pam be visiting your folks?"

"I'll take those blue-edged saucers. They go in the cabinet above the table."

"Elizabeth!" Will cried, hurtling into the kitchen. "Hugh won't let me use Harry's crutches, but he's using them. Why can't I?" His cheeks were flushed and he was blinking rapidly, fighting hard to keep back tears.

"Will, *Harry's* in charge of those crutches. You tell Hugh that I said that Harry decides who can borrow them."

"Yeah, they're Harry's, right? And so should I ask Harry if I can use them?"

"He's the one. But Will, be careful," Lizzie called to his disappearing back. "Remember what happened yesterday when you used the crutches?"

"Too late," Steve said. He put the last mug away and closed the cabinet door. "I'd better check that there are some ice packs in the freezer. He's still got a black and blue forehead from trying to walk with those things."

"While you're there grab the frozen yogurt, and I'll fix cones for the boys."

When he got back, he handed her a frosty quart container. "Why are you giving them yogurt? You know they don't like it. And what about Pam? Won't she be in Philadelphia on Saturday? And didn't she ask us to come down, so that she could see your ring? Something about wanting to see if I'm a cheapskate or not— her words."

"Yogurt's better for them, and they like it as long as you don't tell them it's not ice cream." She began to root through a drawer for the ice cream scoop.

He took her by the shoulders and turned her to face him. "Lizzie, why do I get the feeling that you're ignoring my questions?"

"I told you, it's better for—"

"No," he interrupted. "My other questions. Which leads me to ask if you're ever going to mention to your parents that you're going to be married in a couple months."

She dropped her head against his chest, then looked up at him. "Why are you always right?"

He smiled, pulled her against him, and kissed the top of her head. "I'm not. Actually, it's been statistically proven that you're right ninety percent of the time. This is one of the ten percent times."

"I know." She ran her hands across his back. "I have to tell them, don't I? And you have to meet them. It makes me sick. My father isn't a nice man."

"I've gathered that, but let's think about this for a minute. He isn't violent, is he?"

She sighed. "No, although he can incite violence in others, or at least the desire to do violence. All right." She straightened her shoulders and lifted her chin. "Yes. Pam will be in Philadelphia this coming weekend, so if you're willing, I guess we should get this meeting over with."

"Good. I need to be at the hospital by three. We could get to your folks' place for lunch, if that's okay."

"I'll call."

"When?"

She walked over to the phone.

"Thatta girl." He put the frozen yogurt back into the freezer and took out a half gallon of chocolate chip ice cream. While Lizzie dialed her parents' number, he made three cones and delivered them along with a handful of paper napkins to the boys.

". . .So Saturday's okay, Mother?" Lizzie was asking when he returned to the kitchen. "Probably around eleven-thirty, twelve—and, Mother? There will be five of us. The boys and I and Steven Heller and his son. . . . Yes, he's a friend—well, he's more than that. . .you see, Steven and I are going to be married." She cast Steve a 'help me!' look. "I know. . . .I *know* it's a bit of a shock. . . . Well, Mother, we really don't communicate anymore, since Dad has stopped. . . . All right, we won't get into that. . . . No, he's not a lawyer. . . ." She grinned at Steve. "A son who's Harry's age. . . . Uh-huh, a divorced man. . . No, he's not

Episcopalian—he's Jewish. . . . Well, I already had a church wedding. We thought a garden wedding might be nice . . . ." She laughed. "I don't have much of a garden, Mother, you're absolutely right. Mickey and Harry have dug too many holes, but Steven has—well, maybe not a garden, but a lot of space, and the lawns are nice. . . . We hope in early October. Will you come?. . . .Okay. You'll see when the time comes." She covered her eyes with her hand. "Listen, Mother, we'll see you on Saturday. I love you, Mama."

Steve bent over her chair and kissed the back of her neck. "Thank you, Lizzie. I know it was hard for you, but—"

"It had to be done. I know that."

Traffic was heavy on the turnpike. "Shore-goers," Steve said.

Hugh sighed. "Lucky them." He sat slouched in the back seat, clearly dejected. All three boys were neatly dressed in creased khaki pants, dress shirts, and jackets. Polished penny loafers had replaced their beloved sneakers. Not a recipe for Saturday fun, as far as Hugh was concerned.

Steve looked in the rear view mirror at him. "But think—they aren't going to the Philadelphia Zoo, which, I hear, you guys are. Right, Harry?"

"Right, Steve—with Aunt Pam. Which is way cool, 'cause she'll buy you anything you want, won't she, Hugh?"

"Yeah. . .but first we have to eat lunch."

As they approached Philadelphia, Lizzie fished a Walkman out of her bag and put on the headphones.

"What's this?" Steve asked. "A motivational pep talk?" She held the headphone to his ear. He gave her a questioning look.

"The Brandenburg Concertos. If only I could get away with wearing these through lunch."

Following her directions, he left Route 95 and cut across the northern end of Philadelphia to Chestnut Hill.

"Hey, Steve, that's where Mom went to school." Hugh leaned forward and pointed to an imposing Tudor mansion surrounded by sweeping lawns and a high iron fence.

"Hmm," Steve said. "Kept her fenced in, did they?"

Hugh laughed. "It's called Saint Hilda's. Aunt Pam got thrown out of there."

"Is that right? How'd that happen?"

"This is it, Steven. The driveway is up ahead on the left."

He swung the car between stone pillars, followed a short, curved drive, and pulled into a courtyard fronting a stately Georgian home. Sunlight shimmered through over-arching branches onto its slate roof and a lawn where, he was sure, any errant blade of grass would be quickly rehabilitated or yanked out.

Before following Lizzie and the boys to the house, he stood a moment looking up at its washed brick exterior, trying to imagine Lizzie there as a young girl. "Well," he said, "here we are."

34

LUNCH

AT THE FRONT ENTRANCE LIZZIE RANG THE BELL. A tall, white-haired man opened the door, and for a moment, Steve thought she had badly misread her father. The man had a Santa Claus face without the mustache or beard. His eyes twinkled behind rimless spectacles, and when he smiled, a network of tiny wrinkles turned his face into a map of delight. "Miss Elizabeth!"

"Charles, it's really good to see you." She hugged him, and Steve could see the bond of affection between them.

A butler, he thought, a real goddamn butler. He and the boys followed Lizzie into a spacious hall that was paneled to chest height in gleaming cherrywood and rescued from gloom by the sunlight streaming through two-story-high windows. Several dark oils of somber men in gilded frames hung on the walls. To the left of the entrance a curving staircase immediately fascinated Will, who ran over and peered up.

"You remember the boys, Charles."

"Of course I do." He placed a hand on their heads. "You've both grown quite a bit since I last saw you. But look at you, Master Harry, on crutches. I heard about your adventure."

The boys shook hands with him. "It's okay," Harry assured him. "My leg's almost already healed."

Lizzie introduced Steve and Will.

"Hey, guys, you don't look to me like you're dressed for a trip to the zoo." Pam came running down the staircase.

"Are we allowed to slide down that banister, Aunt Pam?" Will asked, anticipation written on his upturned face.

"Not if you value your life, little guy. You must be Will, Harry's brother-to-be, am I right?"

"Yes, I am, and Hugh's brother-to-be, too."

"Of course, and my nephew-to-be." She spread kisses among them. "Mother's having a nervous breakdown and will be a few minutes."

Lizzie raised her eyebrows.

"She'll be okay. Dad's not home, and Mother thinks it's the end of the world."

They walked down the hall into a room with a beamed ceiling. A massive stone fireplace faced them, and along one wall French doors opened onto a wide stone terrace. Two of the largest Oriental rugs Steve had ever seen covered the floor, their intricate patterns and jewel-like colors worn to antique richness. There were camel-backed sofas and chairs with graceful legs to sit on, and piecrust tables held a multitude of framed photographs, several, he noted, of men in judge's black robes.

"Can we go out back, Aunt Pam?" Hugh asked. At her nod, the children slipped through the doors to the terrace.

"Charles is bringing sodas for the boys," Pam said, "and wine for the grown-ups, but he can get whatever you'd like. Now, let me see this beautiful ring—oh, it *is* beautiful." She held her sister's hand and studied the single round diamond set in a wide gold band. She gave a satisfied nod of her head. "Okay, Steve, you're out of the cheapskate corner. This is a ring with class."

"Thanks, Pam, I appreciate your approval rating."

A short, slight woman quietly entered the room and after pausing momentarily, came over to Steve. "You must be Lizzie's. . .fiance. Dr. Heller?"

He took her outstretched hand in his. "Please, it's Steve, Mrs. Ward." She was older than Steve had expected, shorter than Pam and Lizzie, and painfully thin. Her fair hair was pulled back, leaving her face especially vulnerable with eyes that peered cautiously out at a world she seemed ill-equipped—or perhaps unwilling—to deal with.

"You're very welcome here, and, of course, to our family. I must apologize. . .my husband. . .it's not like him. . . ." She turned to Lizzie. "Elizabeth, dear," she said, taking Lizzie's face in fragile hands.

Lizzie hugged her. "Mama, how are you?"

"Oh, Elizabeth, I'm just a little bit worried about your father. I hope he's all right."

"I'm sure he's fine." She slipped a protective arm around her mother and moved her toward a sofa. "Let's sit and relax. We have lots of catching up to do."

Charles served wine, and they talked until he reappeared to ask Alice Ward about lunch. When she seemed unable to make a decision, Pam spoke up. "We should go ahead, Mother. The boys are probably hungry, and Steve has an appointment downtown later this afternoon."

"Yes, I suppose you're right. I can't imagine what's keeping William."

They had just gotten seated around the dining room table when voices could be heard in the foyer.

"Well, well." William Ward paused in the doorway, letting his eyes rest on each of the faces turned to him. He paused longest when he came to Steve and, Steve noticed, skipped Lizzie entirely. He was tall, a man of military bearing in white shirt, dark tie, and navy blazer. No dress-down Saturday for him, Steve thought. His gaze was direct, even intrusive, but his blue eyes, so like Lizzie's, were washed pale with age. His features were hers too, but it took Steve a moment to see the resemblance, because of his mustache and because all of his facial lines seemed poised in anger.

"Well, well, I forgot we were having company. You'll forgive me." He took his seat at the head of the table, giving his napkin a brisk shake before settling it on his lap. "I see the boys are here. How are you young men? Hugh, what was your final mark in History?" He skewered Hugh with a sharp look.

The boy, caught in the spotlight, stammered. "B-b. . . B-plus, sir."

"You can do better than that. You know you'll need A's to get into Yale. How about you, Harry? All A's?"

"No, Grandfather." Harry reluctantly turned his attention from a plate of rolls and pastries and smiled at Ward. "We don't get grades, just reports."

"Ah, I forgot. Your mother has you in one of the more liberal schools. And who might you be, young man?" He peered closely at Will, taking in the boy's hearing aid. Raising his voice, he asked, "Can you hear me?"

"Yes, I can hear you, William, but I can't read your lips very good, because of your mustache." Will frowned at Ward's full, white mustache, unaware that he had everyone's attention.

"What did you call me?"

"William, same as me. We have the same first name, but my last name is Heller. I'm Steve's boy." He smiled at Steve, who sat opposite and was regarding him with unconcealed affection.

"Well, your father should teach you not to call your elders by their first names."

"You're right, Mr. Ward. I have to confess, it's a lesson I didn't teach," Steve said.

William Ward looked sharply at him, then called to an elderly woman, who was peering through a swinging door with an inquiring expression. "Rose, you may begin to serve."

As the woman filled their bowls with ladles of vichyssoise from a tureen on the sideboard, Lizzie said, "Dad, this is Steven Heller, and you've met his son Will."

Ward turned to Steve. "Mr. Heller, here from New York, are you?"

"Steve is a doctor, William," Alice Ward said in a diffident voice. "From Port Smith."

"Oh, a doctor. I see. Should I call you *Doctor* Heller?" He flashed a quick smile.

Steve returned the smile. "You may, if you like, although you're welcome to call me Steve."

"Aha. Well, thank you. . .Steve. What kind of doctor are you?"

"An MD." He waited while Rose set a bowl in front of his host. "Lizzie tells me that you practice law."

"I'm sure she mentioned that. Her husband was a lawyer, an excellent lawyer, but. . .you probably know that."

"May I have a roll. Please?" Harry asked.

"Of course, dear," Alice Ward said. "Why don't you take one and pass them to Will."

An uncomfortable silence fell as Rose served the soup. The homey sounds issuing from the kitchen made the stillness seem all the more painful, and Steve longed to be finished with the visit and out in the warmth of the August afternoon.

"How's the summer going, Liz?" Pam asked.

"Oh, yes, summer," Ward said. "The educator's reward for having worked all those long five-hour days. Summer and every holiday on the books. Does that describe your job, Steve? It doesn't mine. I guess we chose the wrong professions."

Lizzie stared at her soup for a moment, then smiled at Pam and replied, "It's good, Pam. We missed Nantucket, but we'll go next summer. And being home gave Hugh the opportunity to attend baseball camp."

"Hugh," Pam said, "I hear your team won its division again this year. Are you still pitching?"

"Some of the time. I play outfield, too."

"I'm going to get to one of your games next year. That's a promise."

"That'd be great, Aunt Pam. Sometimes we play on Fridays, so you could come for a weekend. Steve got to our championship game, didn't you, Steve?"

"I did. He's a real good ballplayer, Pam."

"And next year I'll be at the games," Will said. "Just like I got to go to Elizabeth's church and see Harry in that play. Remember, Harry?"

"And where do *you* go to church, Master William?" Ward asked.

"I don't go to church. Neither does my gramma or my grandpa or Dad, do you Dad?"

"No, but we do go to synagogue now and then. Remember we went for Aunt Lorraine's wedding."

"Synagogue?" Ward looked sharply from Will to Steve. "You're Jewish? Heller is a Jewish name?"

"I guess it has to be," Steve said. He moved to allow Rose to serve his lunch plate. "Thank you, Rose." Turning back to Ward, he added, "But, yes, I am Jewish, as far back as I know."

William Ward was silent for a spell, allowing the others to converse about their plans for the afternoon. Alice agreed to go shopping with Lizzie. Pam and the boys were off to the zoo, and Steve was going to the hospital.

"I can drop you off," Pam offered Steve.

"Okay, then Lizzie could take *my* car."

Ward lifted his head with an impatient jerk. "What is this 'Lizzie' business? I believe her name is Elizabeth."

No one spoke. Steve, who looked more surprised than offended, finally said, "Names are a personal matter, Mr. Ward—don't you think?"

Lizzie rose abruptly, her napkin falling to the floor. "Excuse me, please."

Hugh, at Steve's right, gave a tug on his sleeve, and whispered,

"She's sick."

"Excuse me, I'll see if she's all right," Steve said.

He followed the sounds in the hall, and found Lizzie in a powder room, bent over the toilet. He ran cool water on a guest towel.

She straightened and flushed the toilet. "I should have warned you—when I said Dad made me sick, I meant literally sick."

He wiped her eyes and mouth with the damp cloth and waited while she bent over the sink and sloshed water in her mouth.

He handed her a dry towel. "Okay?"

"Okay, I guess." She put her arms around him, and they held each other.

"You don't have to go back in there."

"Umm, I think I do. The boys, you know, and Mother. I was about to say I'm used to it, but. . . ." She shrugged.

Over dessert, Alice asked Lizzie, "What have you been doing with yourself, dear, since you didn't get to Nantucket?"

"There's always so much to do, Mother. Harry and I have been going into the city for his check-ups and physical therapy. And then there are all the preparations to make for the wedding."

Ward glanced quickly at her and then away. "Which wedding would that be?"

"Lizzie," Steve said, "I think it's time for the boys to get into their zoo clothes. They're in the trunk of the car, aren't they?"

"Yes, that's a good idea. Hugh, you can get them. Change in the bathroom downstairs, so Harry doesn't have to do the steps. And give the little boys a hand, won't you, Hugh?" She took the key Steve handed her and gave it to the boy.

After the children disappeared down the hall, Steve turned to William Ward, who sat ramrod straight in his chair, hands curled into fists on either side of his plate, eyes narrowed, a muscle jumping along his jaw line.

"You weren't here before lunch, Mr. Ward, so you missed our conversation. Lizzie and I are going to be married in October."

The silence, broken only by the chattering voices and laughter of the boys coming from the front of the house, was a weight pressing down on them, making speech an effort.

"No, I don't believe this," Ward finally said. For the first time since he had entered the room, he turned to Lizzie. "Your husband is barely dead, and you're going to get married? What will he say?"

His eyes bored through her. Across from her, Alice Ward was clutching her napkin in thin hands that shook. Pam sat toward the edge of her chair, eyes darting between her sister and father.

"Three years last month, Dad," Lizzie said quietly, turning to meet his glare. "Bo has nothing to say about this, because. . .he's dead."

Rising, Ward leaned forward, his hands flat on the table before him, and declared in tones that Steve could imagine filled courtrooms, "Well, *I* have something to say about—"

"No!" Lizzie pounded both fists on the table, shaking the cups in their saucers. "*No—you don't!*"

He stared at her, his lips quivering. "You're going to marry this. . .this *Jew?*" he shouted.

Lizzie stared back at him. Steve, seated to her right, could see that her head, held under such tension, was shaking. He rested a hand on her thigh and was about to speak when she turned to her mother. "Are you ready. . . to go shopping, Mama?" Her voice was as unsettled as the china she'd disturbed.

35

LOVER

HE WAS STRETCHED OUT IN BED, trying to concentrate on material for the gerontology study, with Will finally asleep down the hall, when the phone rang. Expecting someone from his service, he was surprised to hear Lizzie's voice. They'd arrived back in Aspenhill later than they planned, all of them worn out from the trip.

"Steven? Were you asleep?"

Sleep seemed a long way off. Though the meeting at the hospital had gone well, reassuring him that he and Sam were as well prepared as the big city doctors, lunch at the Wards' had his mind racing. He'd known that things weren't wonderful between Lizzie and her father, but he was still surprised by Ward's attack. Nor had he dreamed that Lizzie's family had that sort of money, even if

Lizzie's relationship with her father meant she wouldn't be looking to inherit any of it. Steve himself had probably taken care of that simply by being Jewish.

"No, just catching up on some reading. You okay?"

"Is Will asleep?"

"Yeah, at last. He was really flying."

"Is your front door locked?"

"It doesn't have to be."

"Good. Angelica's here. I'm going to get on my bike and pedal over there."

He laughed. "Okay–pedal carefully."

Ten minutes later he heard her on the steps. She paused in the doorway; if her voice on the phone had sounded free of stress, her eyes and mouth were heavy with it. He pushed journals aside and inched over to make room for her.

She sat on the edge of the bed and leaned against him, her arms going around his neck.

"You did good, Lizzie. We're okay," he whispered into her hair.

They sat quietly for awhile.

"I tried to warn you," she said.

"You did."

"Will's not afraid of him, and Harry's oblivious."

"That leaves you and Hugh and me."

"Umm. What should we do about the wedding? I'd love Mother to be there, but. . . ."

"Would she come with Pam?"

"Maybe. . .I don't know."

"We'll talk to Pam."

"Did you know I love you? Did I ever tell you that?"

"Yeah, you mentioned it."

"Did I tell you why?"

"Nope. Just that you were fond of me." He blew into her hair, breathing in the citrus smell of her shampoo. "Why do you love me, Lizzie Donnelly?"

She wriggled out of his arms and settled against the pillows beside him, stretching her legs along side his. "Here's why. Because your face lights up when you see my sons, and you never cheat when we play gin rummy. Because you listen to me even when I should shut up. Also, I love you because you're a good—no, an excellent—kisser, because the skin right above your hip bones is as soft as—"

"Okay, okay, I never knew I was that lovable. But you know what? I'm also hungry. If you'll put on a pot of coffee, I'll cut you a big piece of Mom's pie."

"Caffeine and sugar. . .right before you go to bed? You should know better."

"I'm really hungry."

"What kind of pie?"

"Blueberry."

She sighed. "Okay. Little pieces, though."

Over large wedges of Barbara Heller's blueberry pie and mugs of hot coffee, they sat in the kitchen and discussed the visit to Philadelphia.

"So mealtime was always an ordeal?"

"Only when we had to eat with Mother and Dad. But, yes, we had to put up with the third degree about everything— school, politics, our friends. I hated it."

Steve pushed his empty plate away, shaking his head.

"But we had Grandmother Ward. She was our safe harbor. Did I tell you that she left the Nantucket house to Pam and me? It's probably why I love to go there. I always feel close to her in that house. And you know what?" she asked, taking the last bite of pie on her fork.

"What's that?"

"I might have had the nanny, the big house, the private schools, but you had the privileged childhood. You had parents who loved you for what you were, and you had your mom's blueberry pie. Now, that's privilege."

"Yeah, you're right. Couldn't lose with all that pie going for me." He leaned over and kissed her mouth. "Just cleaning up the blueberries. You're really staying the night?"

"Umm, only I have to be out of here before Will's up—and I have to be home before Harry's up. Hugh—"

"Lizzie—let's go to bed."

She said, "You know, there's something I want to tell you. . .no, forget it."

"Uh-uh. I believe there's a law that says you can't do that."

"Do what? What law?"

"Start something, then say 'forget it.' You can't do that."

"Really?"

"Really. Tell me."

"It's no big deal. Just that I've been thinking that when we get married, I'll be losing. . . ." She stopped.

"What are you going to lose?"

"Since that night. . .that first night we made love—you remember?"

He nodded in the dark. "Yes, I do."

"Well, ever since that night, I've thought of you as. . .as a lover." She raised herself up and, leaning on one elbow, gazed down at him.

He saw the tears blur his vision before he felt them. She leaned down and kissed him gently on the lips, then on his wet eyelids. She lay back down, settling her head on his chest.

"But you see what I mean. 'Husband' is good—it's great, but I'll have to say good-bye to 'lover.' It's okay, I guess, just sad."

"No."

"No?"

"No. I can be husband *and* lover. It's allowed."

"Is that right?"

"Very right."

"That's another reason I love you. You know all the important rules."